The Mercy Seat

Also by Elizabeth H. Winthrop

The Why of Things
December
Fireworks

The Mercy Seat

A Novel

Elizabeth H. Winthrop

Grove Press
New York

FIRST EDITION

Published simultaneously in Canada
Printed in the United States of America

First Grove Atlantic hardcover edition: May 2018

This book was set in 11.5 pt Scala
by Alpha Design & Composition of Pittsfield, NH

ISBN 978-0-8021-2818-8
eISBN 978-0-8021-6568-8

Grove Press
an imprint of Grove Atlantic
154 West 14th Street
New York, NY 10011

Distributed by Publishers Group West

groveatlantic.com

18 19 20 21   10 9 8 7 6 5 4 3 2 1

For Adin

In memory of Mark

"And the mercy seat is waiting
And I think my head is burning
And in a way I'm yearning
To be done with all this weighing of the truth
An eye for an eye
And a tooth for a tooth
And, anyway, I told the truth
And I'm not afraid to die."

—Nick Cave, "The Mercy Seat"

The Mercy Seat

PART ONE

Lane

When Lane comes out of the gas station store, the dog is waiting for him. It sits in the dusty crossroads, alert and eager, ears pricked and black tongue stiff between its panting jaws. It looks like some kind of ridgeback–pit bull mix, all sinewy muscle and worried brow, like the one he'd had as a kid until his father one day shot her in the cane fields out back, damned if he'd shelter a dog who, during domestic contests, favored the woman of the house. The dog hadn't died right away; Lane had fixed her up as best he could and made her a bed out in the woodshed, where he'd brought her food and water and tended to her wound until she'd disappeared a few days later, likely wandered off to die.

The dog rises nimbly from the dust and turns a circle, follows behind as Lane makes his way to the truck, which is parked in the only shade, beneath a tree. Lane stops and turns. He looks at the dog, then back at the store, a squat, white cinder block structure baking in the crossroads' heat. The battered window shades inside are drawn against the late afternoon sun, and the chipped letters of the TEXACO logo painted on the glass repeat themselves in shadow on the ripped canvas beneath. Lane wonders if the dog is a stray or if it belongs to the people here, to the black-haired woman behind the counter who'd wordlessly taken his money, to the man now coming through the garage door, his shirtsleeves rolled up around grease-stained arms. The woman's husband, Lane would guess; he'd seen living quarters through the door behind the counter, smelled stewing meat.

Lane clears his throat. "He y'all's?" he calls.

The man spits as he crosses to the pump, where a car is waiting for service, shakes his head no.

Lane tosses the dog a piece of the jerky he bought with the coins Captain Seward allowed him and continues to the truck, a bright red 1941 International Harvester cornbinder. Everything about it seems to Lane round in some way: fat round wheel fenders, round hood, round taillights and headlights, as if the whole thing were surprised. And maybe it would be, if it knew what was inside the sheet-metal trailer mounted to its bed. Lane had seen them load it up back at Angola, the straight-backed wooden chair that would have looked innocuous enough but for the leather straps along the arms and the wooden rail between its two front legs. He'd been confounded by the sight; he'd expected some kind of metal contraption with wires and knobs attached. The fact that the chair looks frankly like a chair is troubling to Lane; he finds something deeply sinister in its simplicity.

He opens the truck door and climbs in behind the wheel.

Seward is in the passenger seat, an unlit cigar between his puffy lips. He's a big, chinless man, with a neck so thick his head seems less to sit upon than grow out of it, like a parakeet's.

Seward glances at Lane across the gear shift. "Thought you might have made a run for it," he says. The cigar waggles between his lips as he speaks.

Lane looks at the empty fields around them, the intersecting gravel roads that stretch flatly away: east, west, north, south, anywhere. "Nowhere to go."

Seward gestures at the bag of jerky. "Satisfied?"

Lane offers Seward a piece of the dried meat in reply.

The fat man pinches the cigar from his mouth and exhales as if he's taken a drag. "Too damn hot to eat," he says, but he takes the jerky from Lane anyway, rips a bite off with his side teeth.

It is too hot to eat, a merciless Indian summer, but when they'd stopped so Seward could stretch his bad leg Lane claimed hunger all the same, just as he claimed a need for the facilities when they passed the station before this one. Six years he's been inside, dreamed of things like jerky, M&M's, porcelain underneath his thighs. Now, a prison trusty, he is out, chauffeur to Seward and his chair, and he wants his jerky while he can have it. Wants to want it; its terms make this taste of freedom bittersweet. "Never too hot for jerky when all you've ate for years is gruel," Lane says, though the piece he takes for himself he only plays with, twisting the hardened meat between his fingers. Finally he tosses it in the direction of the dog, who sits by the truck's open door. "Reminds me of the one I had when I was a kid," he says.

Seward grunts. "When you was a kid. What, you a man now?"

Lane says nothing. He's twenty-four years old. He watches the dog eat the jerky, then, from his seat behind the wheel, makes as if to kick the creature. "Git!" he says, as the dog backs away. "Git!" He slams the truck door closed, and the captain and trusty again are under way.

Dale

Dale watches the truck disappear down the road to the south as he fills the tank of the waiting car. The truck kicks up a cloud of dust that hangs behind it in a slowly fading column. It's been a dry spell, October, not a drop of rain in weeks.

He lowers his eyes; vapors shimmer around his hand as the gas tank fills. The numbers on the pump dial tick slowly upward, and with a click, as he releases the handle, at twenty-five they stop. He replaces the nozzle, twists the gas cap shut.

"Quarter," he says, bending through the car's open window. Three glistening faces look back at him: father, mother, and between them on the bench seat, a little girl, country folk in a borrowed or hard-earned car. An infant lies sleeping in a basket in the back.

The driver drops two dimes and a nickel into Dale's waiting hand, as soiled with grease as the man's is with dirt from the field. "Reckon that'll get us far as Houma?"

"Ought to." Dale stands. He puts the hand with coins into his pocket and watches the car drive away, into that lingering column of dust. Then he turns, walks across the boiling lot toward the store. The dog has settled in the shade of the water oak where the truck had parked, not their dog but becoming so after two-odd weeks around. They've never been dog people, but Ora says she can't help feeding him as long as he's here, even as Dale tells her that the fact of her feeding him is why he sticks around.

The bell on the shop door clatters as he pushes inside. It's as hot inside as out, but at least there's a fan. Ora's on a stool behind the counter, her black hair damp against the side of her face. She looks up from her magazine, expectant, and Dale realizes he has nothing to offer, nothing to say; he just came in to come in. He runs a hand through his hair, which is stiff with sweat and dust, leans against the cooler. "Smells good," he says.

"Mmmm."

Dale looks at his wife; she returns his gaze with a stony face.

"Venison?" he asks.

She looks back at her magazine. "Pork."

"That hog's gone a long way."

"Mmm."

"You cool enough?" He offers, "I can move the fan closer."

"I'm all right." She doesn't look up.

"Changed the spark plugs on the truck," he says. "I'm hoping that'll do the trick."

She looks up, her face a question.

"Engine kept misfiring," he explains.

She is uninterested, looks back at her magazine.

Dale pats his chest pocket for his cigarettes, and finds he's left his pack in the garage. He scratches his head, staring at his wife as intently as she's staring at her magazine, her eyes not traveling across the page.

Finally she looks up. "What?"

"What you?" he asks.

She closes her magazine and stands. "Meat's about done," she says, and she goes into the back, shuts the door behind her.

Dale rubs his eyes. He pulls himself from the cooler and crosses to the doorway. He stands there in the glass and stares into the distance, where the highway disappears in a quivering mirage.

Ora

In the kitchen, Ora turns the burner down and without stopping to even lift the lid and look inside the pot, she hurries to the back screen door, which used to slap shut in a familiar sound until last week Dale put felt pads in the door frame. The silence seems louder to Ora than the crack of wood on wood echoing across the field ever did; it makes her uneasy. Used to be that the Negro boy out between the rows of cotton would have looked up at the sound and seen her standing there; now, unaware of her presence, he countinues picking, and puts the cotton into a burlap sack.

She settles on the three wooden steps that lead from the door down into the station's backyard, where it comes edge to edge with the field. Cicadas buzz like rattlers. She wonders if Dale is still leaning against the cooler inside, staring at the place where she was as if he still might get whatever answer he's looking for from the space she'd filled. She doesn't let herself wonder where Tobe is. There hasn't been a letter from Guadalcanal in weeks. She and Dale do not talk about it, as if acknowledging the fact might make its portent real. It is not lost on her how their son's absence, after all these years, has caused the same sort of rift between them as his arrival into their lives did eighteen years ago. Then, they secretly wished for their old life back, each quietly blaming the other for its loss; now they await the mail and news of the Pacific front in anxious silence.

She glances up at a commotion of bird noise, watches a sparrow chase a hawk across the field. From the other side of the building she can hear a car whizzing past on the highway, and then a minute later she can see it, growing smaller down the road to the east. Sometimes Ora finds it strange to live at a crossroads, where almost everyone she sees is going somewhere, while her life is such that she has nowhere to go. When Tobe was younger and would sit with her behind the counter, before he was old enough to pump or be of use to Dale in the garage, they'd make up stories about the people who'd come into the store: the woman in the hat was going to New Orleans for her birthday; the family with the twin babies was moving out to California; the man with the handkerchief was a fugitive from the law. She doesn't make up stories anymore; she only wonders.

The boy in the field has come near to the end of the row, shirtless and sweating. He's maybe nine or ten years old, one of many Negroes who live in tiny tenant shacks on the surrounding land, who conduct their lives as if Dale and Ora's station did not exist. They've got no need for gas and they get their goods from the plantation commissary a couple of miles away. For the twenty years since Dale inherited the station from his uncle and they'd moved up from New Orleans it has been this way. At first Ora thought that surely things would change after they took the station over. She had visions of it as a kind of meeting place, a hangout for both blacks and whites, like the country store in Natchez where she grew up. But Dale didn't share this vision, still doesn't, and nothing's changed at all; the "Whites Only" sign Dale's uncle hung still hangs on the door. It's always added to Ora's sense of isolation here to be surrounded by a whole community and yet to be so thoroughly apart. And Tobe's absence has made that sense of isolation even worse.

Impulsively, Ora calls to the boy, Dale be damned. He looks up at the sound of her voice and drops his hands to his sides, one hand empty, the other wrapped around the top of the sack. He waits. Ora kicks off her sandals and walks through the dirt to the edge of the field. He watches her distrustfully.

"You hungry?" she asks him.

He doesn't answer.

"Got some pork on the stove," she says. "Too much. Bring you a pail?"

"No ma'am." The boy glances over his shoulder, across the field, where others are picking in the distance.

"Not hungry?" she asks.

He turns back to her and shrugs, and beneath the dark skin his shoulder blades rise like bird bones.

"How about some chocolate?"

The boy's eyes flicker. He doesn't refuse.

Ora reaches into her pocket for a half-eaten box of Milk Duds. She shakes a few into her palm and looks at the boy: yes?

He sets his bag down and meets Ora at the edge of the field. She drops the candy into his waiting hand; he looks at the small brown balls with guarded interest.

"Taste one."

He puts one of the candies into his mouth, and as he chews his face registers surprise. "Ain't chocolate," he says.

11

"Caramel inside."

The boy swallows. "I ain't never had chocolate like that before."

There is a shout from across the field; the boy looks again in that direction. Then he turns back to Ora, looking at her as if for permission, or release.

"Go on," she says, and she waves her hand. He puts the rest of the Milk Duds into his pocket, and as she watches him hurry through the dirt clods she is sure that Dale is also watching from the doorway behind her, is sure she feels his disapproving gaze. But when she turns, the doorway is empty, and she is alone.

Dale

Dale goes behind the counter to drop the coins from his pocket into the cash register, and though Ora always gets it right, he has to push the cash drawer in three times before it latches. Beside the register he sees the magazine that Ora has left out on the counter, a copy of *Life* from August, the cover a photograph of a uniformed army officer kissing a well-dressed woman on the cheek. The caption reads "A Soldier's Farewell." Dale blinks. He thinks of January, when the three of them piled into the Bantam and silently drove down to New Orleans, Ora trembling, Tobe resolute, Dale himself hardened against any emotion at all. He can picture the boys gathered against the curb when they got there, waiting for the bus that would take them off to training. They wore blue jeans, not uniforms. Their mothers wept. Their fathers, for the most part, looked uncomfortable. Dale had been. He gazes down at the magazine cover, the uniformed man, the stoic woman. "A Soldier's Farewell" indeed.

The bell sounds above the door, and when Dale looks up he sees that Benny Mayes has arrived for his shift to man the pump by night. The boy is Tobe's age, the youngest of Art Mayes's ten, all of them brought up on land a few miles over that Art still farms at eighty. "Just lettin' you know I'm here," Benny says.

Dale nods in greeting, turns the magazine over cover side down. "You're early," he says. "Ain't yet six o'clock."

Benny shrugs. "Nothin' else to do," he says. He approaches with a paper bag, which he hands to Dale across the counter. "Ma sent these," he says. "Figs. Got a couple of trees busting with 'em."

Dale takes the bag. "Thank her for me," he says.

"She's happy to be rid of 'em."

"Well, happy to have 'em." Dale sniffs. "How's your ma doin'? Ain't seen her lately."

"She's doin' fine."

"Pa?"

"He's all right."

Dale clears his throat. "That nigger working out for him?"

"Seems to be."

"And how's his knee?"

Benny shrugs. "Good enough. He's driving again, anyway. Driving over to St. Martinville tonight to see them execute that boy. Said he wouldn't miss that for the farm."

Dale scratches his head. "Chair'll be inside the jail, is what the paper said. Ain't gonna be much to see."

Benny shrugs, and for a moment, they are quiet.

"Anyway," Benny says, finally. "I'll be out waitin' in the truck."

"Right," Dale says, and watches the boy go.

Lane

On his right hand Lane has a scar, which, when he grips certain things too long, like the handle of an ax or an oyster knife or a steering wheel, begins to burn as if the skin were being pulled apart all over again, and by the time they reach the boggy land along Bayou Teche, the scar has begun to pain him. He'd gotten it at thirteen, the first time he ever punched through a glass window, before he knew to wrap his hand in cloth, before he knew how to pick a lock. That first time it wasn't to steal so much as take back what was rightfully his, a Remington 12-gauge that had belonged to his grandfather, and that his father had wagered in a hand of poker he lost to a fellow cane worker named Guy Davis. Lane had punched through the windowpane above the knob of the kitchen door, reached through the jagged opening in the glass, and just like that, he found himself in another man's home: cold soup on the stove, dirty dishes piled in the sink, mud-caked boots by the door. Left open, the wound had healed poorly, a raised wormy line that reminds him always of how easy it is to break into someone's home.

He shakes his hand out and presses his scarred knuckle to his mouth, tasting the salt of his own sweat. He can't see the bayou from the road, but he can smell its fustiness, a mix of mineral, marsh, and earth that reminds him of home. Sugarcane and cotton fields have given way to pecan groves,

15

which soon give way to the stately, columned homes that cluster among the live oaks on the edge of New Iberia. Here is where they are meant to pass the night after the midnight execution in St. Martinville, twelve miles to the northeast. Seward has fallen asleep in the passenger seat; he breathes throatily, and the way his jaw occasionally snaps makes Lane wonder if the man might be eating in his dreams. It's occurred to Lane that with the captain sleeping he could drive the chair anywhere, or run, but he doesn't know where he'd go and as he's already done half his time, he figures he'd be better off seeing it through than risking a punishment even worse. And now here they are, arriving with their terrible cargo.

Lane glances at the captain. Seward stirs, clears his throat, and rearranges himself in his seat, glancing at Lane as if to gauge whether his slumber has been noticed. Then he unscrews the cap of the flask he keeps in his breast pocket and drinks, and after he's wiped his mouth, he keeps his hand cupped against his face as he peers through the windshield.

Outside, evening sunlight glints in dust motes kicked up by passing traffic: sugarcane wagons and oil trucks, brown tanks on flatbeds. The truck's engine murmurs steadily. "Ain't been to New Iberia since '37," Seward says, finally. He drops his hand. "Year my grandbaby was born and died."

"Year I went to jail," Lane mutters. He thinks he might have passed through New Iberia when his father's pa took sick, but he was a boy and it was the middle of the night and he can't say for sure if it was New Iberia or some other sugar and oil town. He remembers his father talking about oil field trash, and he remembers a field of derricks in the moonlight, a city of spindly rods. Much of the past presents itself to Lane this way, in flashes without context. It's as if his existence before Angola is a series of discrete and dreamlike moments, without a binding narrative: a goose caught up in hog wire, his mother weeping over a soup pot in the side yard, the tiny naked bodies of his siblings in the rain. Of Angola, there is little to remember, with every day the same.

Lane slows the truck when they come to downtown. Until now, the drive has been all swamp, prairie, and cane field, the occasional tiny town. This is the first real city Lane has seen since he was sentenced in Thibodaux six years ago. Men sit in chairs in the shade in front of a barbershop, where a pole spins slowly by the open window. People walk up and down the street, past shopwindows where suited mannequins pose, where books and clocks and pastries are on display. Outside the theater, beneath a blinking marquee, people stand in line for a matinee, fanning themselves with whatever they can find. Lane remembers driving in the prison bus from the courthouse in Thibodaux and looking out at streets like these with longing. Now, looking out the window, he's filled with puzzlement that verges on panic. It's the same as any downtown he's ever seen, but he may as well have landed on the moon. Movies, restaurants, boutiques, fancy shoes: none of it seems to make sense anymore. He wonders if it ever really did.

"Take a left here." Seward points. "Iberia Street."

Lane turns, stopping as Seward instructs him in front of a large white building set back from the street, a four-story cement-stucco structure at the top of a tiered set of concrete stairs, with pilasters between five slitlike window casements that rise nearly to the height of the building. The double doors and window frames are dulled aluminum, the doors imprinted with eight shining, circular disks. It's unlike any building Lane has ever seen.

"Courthouse," Seward says. "Nigger's waiting in there. Cell up top. And I reckon he's not feeling too good tonight, boy."

Lane pauses. The sudden proximity of the convicted man to the chair that will kill him makes Lane feel peculiar. "I thought he was in St. Martinville."

"Hah. They'd a left him in the St. Martinville jail the good townspeople would have done our job for us before we even left Angola."

Lane looks at the building, trying to imagine the man inside, what a man might be doing when he knows he has only a few more hours to live. "What'd he do?" he asks.

Seward spits out the window. "Raped a white girl. In her own bed. Crept right in through the window and had his way with her, with her daddy in the room next door."

Lane pauses again. "He kill her?"

"Kill her? Pah. Don't know if he'd be safe anywhere if he'd a killed her too." Seward pats the side of the truck, his ring clanking against the metal. "Though he may as well have," he adds. "Killed herself soon after. Blew her brains out with her daddy's gun the next day."

Outside, beyond the courthouse, the sky is glowing with the eerie orange hue of burning season, though it isn't. A nearby church bell tolls six times, and it occurs to Lane, as he listens, that the condemned man is hearing the same sound, too.

Willie

There's a dog barking at the edge of the onion field as he and his father work the rows, pulling up the bulbs whose tops have dried. Willie's got a sack full of them, not just white ones but purple, brown, green, even blue. His father is a few rows away, bending, standing, bending, standing. It's sunny, not a cloud overhead, but his father is as wet as if he'd just come from the bayou, his shirt stuck fast to his skin, britches dripping, and when Willie looks down at himself, he sees that he's wet, too; his sleeves are soaked, and droplets shimmer on his shackles.

Willie! His father's voice carries across the rows of onion grass. *Willie!*

He looks up. His father's holding an onion red as blood and big as a basketball, unlike anything Willie's ever seen. His father takes his hat off and waves it at Willie, and as he's holding it in the air an eagle swoops in from overhead and takes it from his hand. Willie lifts his own hand to shield his eyes from the sun, and as he watches the bird soar away, giant talons clutched around the hat brim, he begins to understand that he is dreaming.

He leaves his eyes closed as the dream recedes, stranding him again in grim reality. He holds on to the image of his father, of the onion field, but he can feel the hard cot beneath him, hear the water dripping from the pipe in the corner of his cell, smell the putrid sludge leaking from the base of the seatless toilet. As there was in his dream, there is the sound of a barking dog, always a barking dog.

He opens his eyes and sees the day's last rays falling slatted through the window bars and onto the concrete walls. He hadn't meant to sleep. But these days sleep comes when it comes, and always it brings dreams. Sometimes his dreams are nightmares: seared flesh, scorched hair, lethal currents zinging through his body. But mostly he dreams about little things, like having a splinter underneath his thumbnail, or drawing circles in the dirt with bare toes, or the way you feel you're going to fall when you're running backward to catch a ball coming down against a blinding sun, little details that make sleep feel more like living than wakefulness does. Wakefulness is merely existing. Wakefulness is waiting to die, and waiting for what is happening to seem real.

None of any of it has seemed real, from the moment he first saw Grace, elbow deep in a mixing bowl with flour across her face, a perfect crescent of white just beneath her cheekbone—this image of her is one that for weeks he turned over and over in his mind as he scrubbed tins crusted with cake and bowls sticky with the sweet streaks of batter, or as he walked home from his shift, so lost in his own mind that when he got home he couldn't remember getting there. After that moment, he found himself in a world defined by Grace, a world in which everything seemed a dream: the rush of an accidental touch in the kitchen, the conversations that they held with their eyes, the slight weight of her body above his own, the heady thrill, the terror. And then dream turned nightmare: her father's raging face in the doorway, his own blind sprint home through the predawn streets, the deputies and lynch mob arriving shortly after, both at once, cursing and yelling and pounding on the door. Sometimes Willie wishes the mob had gotten to him first.

He rises from his cot and looks out the window. The sun is nearing the horizon, a smoldering globe, sunk low enough that the tin roofs of the clapboard houses around the parish courthouse, which all day glint in the sun, lie in shadow, though the spire of St. Peter's still rises skyward into light. It's the last of the sun he will ever see. The notion is so strange that it doesn't bother Willie the way he knows it should, the same way he figures shock at first staves off the pain of a broken bone.

After some minutes he is aware of footsteps coming down the hallway, and the sound of jingling keys. Willie breathes deeply, turns from the window, and sits down on the edge of his cot. The sun glows in his vision. The footsteps near.

Sheriff Grazer appears at his cell door, accompanied by a man in brown garb identical to Willie's own. The man waits just behind Grazer, looking at Willie nervously as the sheriff fits the keys into the lock. In his hands the prisoner holds a bowl with a straightedge razor, scissors, brush, and soap.

Grazer swings the cell door open and ushers the inmate inside.

"Evenin', Willie," the prisoner says.

Willie nods, lifting a hand to touch his cheeks, his hair.

Grazer brings a folding chair in from the hallway. "Burl come to clean your head, boy," he says, arranging the chair in the middle of Willie's small cell.

"Sorry, Willie," Burl says, laying the brush, soap, and scissors down on the cot. He's small and wiry, old enough to be gray at the temples but still youthful in body. He looks at Willie regretfully, the whites of his eyes rheumy yellow. Willie nods once, a sign of reassurance or forgiveness. Burl turns to fill the bowl at the sink.

"Have a seat," Grazer says, gesturing Willie toward the chair. Willie rises from the cot. As he sits down on the folding chair he thinks of Maud Clover's barbershop in St. Martinville, how the white men would kick back there for hours under smocks like tents, trading tales with Maud as the barber clipped around their ears or drew his straightedge razor across their sudsy necks. On his way home as a kid some afternoons Willie would stop and talk to Little Maud outside, his eye always only half on Little Maud as, transfixed, he watched through the window the barber's blade slide across a field of stubble, the thrilling balance of pressure as the razor's indentation moved along the flesh, skating precisely along the line between gentle and firm.

Willie feels Burl drag a wet washcloth across his head. He blinks, returning to his cell; so often does he vanish into thought.

"Sure is a nice evenin'," the inmate says, behind him. "I reckon it's getting cooler."

"Oh, we ain't done with the heat," Grazer says. He's leaning up against the wall of the cell in front of Willie, his big arms crossed. "I reckon next week'll be worse than last."

"That right," Burl says.

Willie looks at his hands, touches a cracked spot near the knuckle that has been bothering him some. He thinks how little the weather matters. It will be hotter or cooler next week without him. It's another odd thought. He picks at the spot near his knuckle, draws blood, and thinks of the wound how little it matters, either.

"Well," Burl mutters. He rubs soap into Willie's hair. "That OK, Willie?"

Willie shuts his eyes; the feel of Burl's knobby fingers on his skull is like sinking, worn out, into sleep. "That's fine," he says. It's been some time since he's felt this kind of human touch.

"Got to be clean to see the Lord," Burl murmurs.

Grazer makes a sound: a snort, a scoff. Willie opens his eyes. "You gotta be bald, boy," Grazer says, and he's looking straight at Willie, the side of his mouth up high, "so the electricity can pass right though that thick skull. Ain't got nothing to do with the Lord."

Burl drags the razor across Willie's head. "I reckon you'll be clean, too, Willie," he says quietly. He wipes the razor on a towel, and again Willie shuts his eyes.

Frank

At sundown they're still several miles from St. Martinville when Bess shows signs of tiring, slowing her gait at just the time Frank would otherwise be inclined to crack the switch by her head. But she is an old mule; they're both old. It's hot, too, and already she's pulled the wagon more miles in a single day than she has in the past month, so he respects her pace, even if he could walk the miles home doubly faster.

"S'all right, girl," he murmurs, steering her to the side of the road. "Hold up now, whoa." He tugs back gently on the reins. Bess stops. She blinks slowly, hangs her head, waits.

Frank ties off the reins and climbs stiffly from the bench to the dusty ground. He gets the mule's feed bucket and a steel canteen from the wagon bed, and he pours out what's left of their water, leaving barely enough for himself to splash his face. It's warm, but the water feels good.

Bess lowers her head to drink, but she takes only a sip before pulling away.

"All right, girl." Frank draws his hands down the mule's face, the solid nose bone wide and reassuring. "We be home soon enough," he tells her, looking into her dark eyes. On their surface he can see his own reflection, an old man in his Sunday best.

Frank lifts the bucket and pours the water down the length of the mule's back, then returns the can and bucket to the wagon bed. There, a simple slab of granite lies across the wooden planks, the day's somber cargo fetched from over in Youngsville, about eleven miles to the west from his home in St. Martinville. It cost him eighty-five dollars, most of them borrowed against a failing crop of onion and the promise of odd jobs, but his youngest boy's going to have a headstone if it kills the mule and Frank himself besides. It'll kill Elma if he doesn't. She had wanted him to get it sooner, but getting it seemed to Frank an acceptance of the unacceptable, so he put it off, put it off again, and finally decided on this final day to do it because he didn't know how else he'd fill the hours otherwise. He wouldn't have been able to bear being home with Elma.

Frank rubs his eyes and looks off into the distance. A white field of cotton stretches away, abuzz with the insects of evening, the bursting hoary bolls aglow. This time yesterday he and Elma were telling the boy good-bye. This time tomorrow he'll be gone. Even after months of counting down, of measuring the weeks and days until this time, he still can't fathom it. He figures Elma's done enough fathoming for them both, mourning the boy before he's even gone. Though really Frank figures he was gone before his trial had even begun—figured it in fact from the moment he came home and saw Willie sitting there with his back against the mule shed, the girl's head resting in his lap as the boy ran his fingers through her hair.

In the distance there's the growing sound of an engine, and when Frank looks down the road behind him he sees a pickup truck barreling in from the west, an outline in a glowing cloud of dust. He goes around again to Bess and grabs her reins just below the bit, to soothe her during the noisy passing. But the pickup doesn't pass; instead, some yards away from where Frank has stopped on the side of the road, it slows down, then pulls onto the shoulder.

There are two white men in the cab. Frank eyes them warily, though it's hard for him to see them clearly through the windshield. The passenger side door opens, and a man gets out. He's wearing boots and denim pants, and a baseball cap perches on his head. He approaches Frank slowly, a hand in his pocket. Frank's grip tightens around the reins. He squints in the setting sunlight.

"You doin OK?" the man asks.

"Yessuh, just givin the mule some water, suh."

"Mmmmm-hmm. We seen you pulled over, thought you might have a busted axle or some such."

"No suh. Just about to be on my way."

"Where you headed?"

"Over St. Martinville," Frank says, nodding to the east.

"Be dark 'fore you get there, by the looks of that mule," the man says, eyeing Bess.

"Yessuh, I reckon it will."

"Right then." The man pulls on the brim of his cap and takes a step backward, and then he turns around and goes back to the pickup. He gets inside, and after a moment, the truck pulls into the road and drives away.

Frank watches it disappear in the same direction he will take, his heart galloping from the innate fear he's wished to God so many times that Willie, too, possessed.

Willie

After Burl and Sheriff Grazer have left his cell, Willie lies down on his cot to wait. He'd thought to pick up the Bible Father Hannigan gave him months ago, or one of the magazines the deputies give him when they're finished with them, but it doesn't seem right to read about movie stars when you're about to die, and the stuff in the Bible he doesn't believe, though he's tried—he's read the Bible, he's prayed, he's gone through all the Christian motions, hoping to believe. Wanting to believe. He figures it would make this whole thing easier if he did, but he can find no comfort in religion, in the book his mother lives by. And so he lies on his cot, watching his cell fill with the golden light of evening, just waiting. Waiting: he is tired of it.

He shuts his eyes. Water drips rhythmically from the pipe in the corner of the cell. From down the hall, he can hear radio voices talking in the bullpen and an inmate weeping. Outside, the clock bells sound; it is six-thirty. Five and a half more hours. Something briefly slices through his body: the hint of a shiver, maybe; the trace of a tremor. But it is so slight he can't discern its origin: expectation or terror. Maybe both. He is as glad for the waiting to be over as he is frightened of the death he's waiting for.

Willie's known many people who've died. Mo Bunyon's heart stopped cold one day as the old man sat in the shade of an oak tree, his legs crossed and his lip full of dip. Frankie Dunham disappeared in the bayou and Butch Clover got crushed at the mill by a rolling log. But these deaths don't come to mind when Willie considers his own. These are stories, legends, experienced communally and at arm's length, part of his childhood vocabulary. Only once has he actually seen the passage from here to there, and this is what his mind turns to, when he thinks of death, over and over again.

His Uncle Breeze had been dying before their eyes, growing thinner, frailer, reedy-voiced, but somehow they hadn't really noticed. Or Willie hadn't noticed—he was twelve, he was busy, he was a boy—until one day he came home at midday and found Breeze laid up on the couch. Resting, the old man said, but he never once got up again. Willie and Darryl and their parents sat on a stool beside him, taking turns at vigil, giving the old man ice chips, pudding, juice. Willie remembers the man's fattened legs, the way his feet became lost in their own swelling, the brittle foot skin stretched and cracking. He remembers the heat of the fire, those cold, fat feet so cold anyway. He can remember the smell: sweet, rotten, beets and dead mice. He remembers the old man's swollen belly and the strained wheeze, the rasp and rattle of saliva and air in his throat. When it was Willie's turn to watch, he was afraid to look away, afraid also of those rare lucid moments when his uncle's eyes would open and, back from wherever he'd gone to, Breeze would have something to say. Those moments had terrified Willie, but the aftershocks of death had terrified him more, the shuddering of the lifeless body. After that, any notion Willie had of death as something peaceful was gone.

He tries not to imagine Grace's death. But sometimes the visions come to him unbidden: her blond hair matted with blood, the shattered skull, the crimson pool spreading beneath her, her lips—which hours before had been against his own—gone slack around the gun. And when these visions come, it is all Willie can do not to beat his head against the concrete walls of his cell, his soul aching with regret; he ran away. He'd have never let it happen if he'd stayed.

Frank

Bess won't take another step. Frank coaxes her from the wagon bench, but she snorts and stamps a hoof. "Come on, girl, giddap," he says. He reaches for the switch in the wagon bed and holds it by her eye, but the mule makes no attempt to move, and Frank's not going to whip her. He draws a callused hand over his face, then puts the switch aside and climbs back down from the wagon. He tries leading her next, grabbing the reins below the bit and pulling her from the road's shoulder. At this she whinnies, tosses her head, even makes a move to lower herself to the ground, but she's held up by the shaft tugs.

Frank lets go of the reins. He looks at the mule and nods; she is through. Frank thinks he might try to pull the load himself, if he were a younger or a stronger man. He's got a memory of his son Darryl in the weeks before he went off to Lejeune, his hands around the wagon shafts as he hauled loads of melon, *gettin' himself strong*, he said, though Frank reckoned Darryl was strong enough already.

He looks up and down the empty road; there are no headlights, no signs of traffic. Just gravel and the sinking sun. It's why he'd taken this road in the first place, instead of the busier highway that runs mostly parallel to it, and he wishes now he'd asked for help when he had the chance. The bugs are getting louder with evening, screeching in the cotton. His cousin Earl will be waiting, ready to help him set the stone in place. Elma will be waiting, too. And then there's Willie; he wants to see his son once more before he dies, even if it's only from a distance as the boy's transported from New Iberia to the St. Martinville parish jail. Needs to. His pulse quickens at the thought. Part of him wants to leave the wagon, mule, and stone behind and walk the last few miles back to St. Martinville, just to get back, but as much as Elma likely needs him near as the midnight hour approaches, he knows that she would die to see him empty-handed, after she's been on him, on him, on him, to go and get their youngest boy a stone. Their youngest boy, born to them so late, both accident and miracle.

He looks once more up the road, down. Nothing. But on the far edge of the next field up he sees the small, dark shape of a cabin. Tenant farmers, he thinks. Could be they have a mule. And there are still hours till midnight; he's got time.

Father Hannigan

Hannigan stands in the belfry even after the day's final call to prayer has sounded. He wonders how many people in this town have actually dropped to their knees at the sound.

Above him, the bell still swings gently, and though the clapper no longer strikes the rim, the copper still hums. Up and down, the fat rope passes through his loosened grip. Soon, scattered pigeons will return to the bell house sills, and both bell and rope will come to rest. When he was a boy at the orphanage in Pennsylvania he'd ring the bells at church time and the rope would take him with it, and off he'd be on a ride, at the mercy of all that clanging power. That's what he liked about the church as a boy; the power of God was a secondary draw. And down here, in Louisiana, he's found there are greater powers still: poverty and bigotry and fear. In the face of these it sometimes seems to him his mission doesn't stand a chance.

He drops his hand from the rope and leaves the belfry. In the nave, late sunlight falls slantwise through the arched windows and lies broken by the panes in glowing rectangles across the wooden pews and dull linoleum of the floor. St. Edward's is a humble building, nothing like Hannigan's Spiritan base in Pittsburgh, with its soaring ceiling, marble floors, and stained glass. But Hannigan is more at ease inside St. Edward's. He takes comfort in the simple cross on the white east wall, the spare wooden pews, the modest altar. When the church is empty, the space looks small, and so on Sundays he's always amazed by the sea of faithful faces, the multitude of bodies the rows in fact accommodate. In here, he feels at home, that things are right, that humanity has a chance; it is out there on the streets of New Iberia where even after several years he feels he hasn't found his footing, a way of wading through blind hate. The south feels more foreign to him than his mission in Madagascar ever did.

His footsteps are silent as he walks down the aisle toward the open church door. Outside he can see a car parked at the curb, the hanging branches of an oak, the accounting office housed in the low building across the street, kids playing baseball in the ballpark beyond. He thinks of Willie Jones, not much more than a kid himself. His throat tightens.

At the back pew, Hannigan turns to face the altar, and though he doesn't always do so before exiting the church, he kneels to make the sign of the cross before he leaves. He shuts his eyes, and waits, for something, anything. But he feels only the weight of his heart.

When he opens his eyes again, for a moment he stays kneeling there. Then he stands, and though he isn't ready, he steps out into the gathering night. The woman and then Willie are waiting.

Gabe

Darkling beetles have been burrowing, it's been that hot and dry. Far out in left field, Gabe watches one emerge from the dirt near his feet, the hard black body shuddering itself free of the earth, the spindly legs tap-tapping at the ground as the creature begins to make its slow way toward the road. Gabe wonders where the beetle is going, or if the beetle even knows. Lately he's been wondering this kind of thing. It's like the dog across the street, rooting by the trash in the church alley. He's looking for food, probably, but Gabe wonders if the dog knows what he'll do afterward, or if beetles and dogs and squirrels and birds just do what they do while they're doing it, no thought to the past or what comes next.

"Livingstone!"

Gabe looks across the baseball field toward home plate, where the other boys have gathered in the dusk. Kevin Saunders is waving at him. "You comin'?"

Gabe squints at Kevin across the field, and then up at the sky as if for an answer: is he coming? A red-tailed hawk soars above the piney tree line, and Gabe finds himself wondering about the hawk, too.

"Livingstone!"

He looks back at Kevin.

"You comin' or you gonna stand there all night?"

I'm gonna stand here all night, Gabe thinks, but he starts to cross the field, jogging as slowly as he might otherwise walk, his eyes on his feet as they scuff across the ground. He can hear the voices of the other boys as he approaches, snippets of conversation: *Cold Cokes at the pharmacy . . . Old lady Peterson's veranda . . . Rope swing at the bayou.* He hears Chub Larson talking about his mama's brisket, and the Kane twins still arguing over an out. Buddy Cunningham's voice is loudest. Buddy Cunningham's country, but he comes in for games, walking the four miles each way from the land his daddy farms. And *My daddy,* Buddy's saying, *My daddy, come midnight my daddy's going to go to St. Martinville to watch that nigger fry!*

Gabe looks up abruptly, but Buddy's proclamation goes unnoticed. Most of what Buddy says goes unnoticed, the bulk of it uttered just so he might be heard.

It's only later, once a pack of them has reached the main part of town and set up with sodas in the square, that Buddy brings it up again. Chub Larson has gone home, and the Belty brothers, also country, have hitched a ride on Abe Dougie's wagon as far out as the sand pits, anyway. Most of the younger kids, except Berle Williams, who has no rules, have gone home, too. But Kevin, Buddy, the Kane twins, Rud Scott, Caliber, and Gabe, they're all lingering, easing comfortably into the lull of a weekend. Gabe lies on his back in the grass, staring up at the glowing sky through the sprawling branches of a live oak. He watches the day fade, only half listening to the other boys, who are talking about the fire that burned down Hattie LeMay's house. The Kane twins swear it was an accident, Caliber says arson, and Rud Scott's talking about Jewish lightning, when Buddy says, loudly, "You know, I think I may just go with my daddy."

Gabe shuts his eyes. Rud Scott stops in mid-sentence. There's a pause, in which Gabe can hear Rud loudly slurp the dregs of his Coke before responding to the interruption. "And what in the hell does that have to do with the price of eggs, Cunningham?"

There's another pause. "Y'all weren't talking about eggs," Buddy says, finally. Gabe opens his eyes. One squirrel is chasing another in the branches overhead, rustling through the brittle resurrection fern.

"It's a saying, Cunningham."

"Well y'all can say all the sayings you want and while you do that I'm a go with my daddy and watch that nigger fry."

No one responds. Gabe hears the sound of a car engine approach, drive clockwise around the square, and fade in the other direction.

It's Kevin who speaks next. "Whatta you talking about, Cunningham?"

"Nigger over in St. Martinville," Buddy says. "He done raped a banker's daughter. That's what my daddy says. They bringin' an electrical chair over from Angola to fry him up."

"Ain't no such kind of chair," Bill Kane scoffs.

"Is so! And my daddy—"

"It was a baker's daughter, not a banker's daughter. Grace Sutcliffe. And the boy who raped her cleaned the dishes." This is Caliber, at fourteen the oldest of the boys. Gabe looks at him sharply; the older boy is looking directly at him. Gabe feels his face start to burn, and he looks away, willing Caliber to say nothing more. "Except some folks in St. Martinville say it wasn't rape at all."

Buddy Cunningham scoffs. "Well, then, what was it?" he demands.

Caliber shrugs in the mysterious way that he has. "Baker's in the Klan," he says. "He'd call it rape no matter what it was."

Buddy snorts. "Well, whatever it was," he says, "my daddy's goin'. And I'm a go with him."

"Ain't no such kind of chair!" Bill Kane says again. "Is there?"

"Gruesome Gertie," Caliber says gravely. "That's what they call it."

Gabe stares at the branches overhead, which transform in his mind into a grisly scaffolding, a postcard his father once showed him of a human harvest dangling.

For some time, no one speaks. And then Rud Scott clears his throat. "Well," he says. "My pa bets his life that it was Jewish lightning."

Father Hannigan

He passes the rectory on his way downtown. He tells himself that he wants to walk through the park, though in fact he barely notices when for a quarter mile grass replaces pavement beneath his feet, and when he comes to the park's other side, there's Lombard Street just a stone's throw away. He turns onto it automatically, unthinking, drawn there by a force that is irresistible, powerful as he believes God is meant to be: bottled salvation.

The rectory is a small clapboard building, indistinguishable from the other houses that line the residential street except for its coat of paint, which, though no longer fresh, isn't peeling, as the paint on most of the other houses seems to be. Hannigan follows the walkway across the small, dry lawn to the front stoop, where he squints at his ring of keys, searching for the small silver one. Before he opens the door, he pauses and looks at the street around him. Some evenings, there are children out on the pavement, but tonight the street is empty. Only a few cars are parked along the curb, one of them his own, provided by the order. It's an older car—a Ford station wagon with wood siding, wire wheels, and an external horn that no longer works. Inside are traces of the priest from whom Hannigan took the parish over three and a half years ago—his rosary beads in the glove box, and his pair of driving gloves in the well of the driver's side door. Hannigan has left these things where they are, as if that priest might yet return from his new mission in Ceylon and relieve Hannigan of his duties here.

The only person Hannigan sees tonight is the old man who lives several houses down from the rectory. He is sitting on his porch as he always is, oblivious to Hannigan's presence. Hannigan has visited him once before. He sat by the man's feet, on the top step of the porch, and spoke about the weather, and music, and how time passes, and a little bit about God, but the man was silent, and after a while, Hannigan stopped talking. He could smell bacon and something sweet cooking inside, could hear a woman humming, but she never came outside, and he wasn't invited in.

Hannigan salutes the man tonight, but his gesture goes unnoticed, or ignored. He unlocks the rectory door and steps inside, and he's greeted immediately by the distinct smell of the place, an unnamable scent which if pressed to describe he'd say was a curious combination of rain, dirt, and basil. When he first moved here from Madagascar, he found the smell irksome and distracting, but he's come to take comfort in it, its sourcelessness and mystery.

He puts his hand on the switch of the lamp by the door, then hesitates, imagining the sudden yellow that will spring forth from the bulb when he turns it on. Now, the room around him is blue with evening: the small sofa, the coffee-table trunk, the white walls, the wood floor. Particles seem to spill from the hazy borders of different objects and mingle in the blue air, as if with night everything will slowly become one. His mother called this hour the gloaming, and when he was a boy, the word frightened him. It's one of the odd and precise things he remembers clearly of his mother. He also remembers the smell of scallions on her breath, and a red cotton blouse. He remembers the tune of a song she sang, and has a notion that it had to do with strawberries.

He drops his hand from the light switch without turning it on and crosses the room to the kitchen. His coffee and the soggy remnants of this morning's cereal are still out on the small table, where he'd been eating when Jason Biggs came knocking at the door, frantic, his baby stillborn. This morning seems like days ago. Hannigan rubs his eyes, thinking of that tiny dark creature in his palm, the shriveled skin, the fragile bones, and Della Biggs dumb with grief. And what was Hannigan supposed to say? What comfort could he give? His thoughts turn again to his mother, how her grief when his brother died had been too much for her to bear. Five years old, Hannigan had been unable to give comfort then, either, and one death became two, though of each death he remembers nothing but the knowledge that it had occurred. And so his mother exists as the smell of scallions, the tune of a song, and his brother lives in a single vivid image: a boy, crouched on the dusty ground before glass marbles, sunlight catching in each.

Hannigan puts the bowl and mug into the sink, then takes a long drink of milk from the bottle in the icebox. He's eaten nothing since the cereal, and he knows he ought to eat, but when he opens the pantry door and scans the offerings—crackers, canned sardines, onion or tomato soup, peanut butter, applesauce—nothing appeals. Nothing aside from the Old Crow straight rye at the very back of the cabinet, a housewarming gift from the pastor of St. Peter's, still corked and sealed with wax, often thought of and never thrown away. He reaches for it, looks down at the smooth bottle, the little village on the label nestled in some Kentucky valley, the brown liquor inside, for him both poison and saving grace. He considers the bottle, then puts it back, and shuts the pantry door.

Nell

"He ought to be having pork," she says, cracking an egg into a waiting dish. "I asked him when I saw him, I said, What's your favorite food? And he says, without missing a beat, he says, Pork, ma'am, with rice and gravy." She adds a little cream to the egg, then whisks it all together with a fork and puts the bowl into place, so that before her on the counter is a lineup: catfish, cornmeal, egg, breadcrumbs, and then, on the stove, a waiting pan of oil. She brings a match to the burner beneath; it ignites with a whoosh.

"But it being Friday, and him being a good Catholic—or *trying to be*, as he said—he said he wouldn't have any meat but fish." She spears a fillet angrily, rolls it in cornmeal, dunks it in egg, drenches it in breadcrumbs, and sets it in the pan to fry.

She turns around. Mother sits in a chair by the window, a silhouette in the evening light, very still, her head tilted slightly, as if searching for sound in her silence—the sound of Nell's voice, the sound of the concerto playing on the radio on the counter. Her bony hands are curled around the ends of the chair's arms. On the table in front of her, the ice has melted in a glass of iced tea, given to her each evening out of habit, though Nell can't remember the last time the woman took a sip. All she drinks now is milk through a straw, her fallen mouth puckering around the plastic.

"Even if he's guilty, I don't think he should die. But to be true, Mother, I'm not sure anymore that he's guilty at all." The utterance lingers in the air like something tangible, as tangible as its meaning felt inside her gut, poisonous and roiling. *The boy.* A boy, that's what he is; she understood this the moment yesterday when she finally saw him in the flesh—a boy every bit as much as Gabe, just older. She didn't want to meet him; but after months of rankling unease, something in her finally had to. "And if he's not, well, may heaven forgive your son."

Mother stares out the window, unhearing. Nell smells the catfish burning on the stove.

Polly

If he's read it once, he's read it a thousand times, the warrant he chased after, sentencing Willie Jones to *a current of electricity of sufficient intensity to cause death, and the application and continuance of such current through the body of the said Willie Jones until said Willie Jones is dead.*

Still, Polly reads it one more time, stares at it. The document sits on his desk, atop a desk pad on which he's scribbled endless geometric shapes, one against the next in an ever-expanding city of them that grows according to his nerves. He holds his hand over his mouth, chin in palm, elbow on desk, staring at the words beneath him as if they somehow might change. He taps the fingers of his free hand on the desktop, a gentle galloping thud, three beats for each tick of the mantel clock. It's getting dark outside, and city hall has mostly emptied for the night; the clerks and accountants and the mayor have all gone home. His office is getting dark, too; when he sat down, afternoon sunlight was streaming in through the window, so he didn't bother with the lights, and even now that the sun has set he still hasn't bothered.

He lifts his eyes from the document before him only when the phone at the edge of his desk begins to ring. His mind springs to the possibility of an eleventh-hour reprieve, but that hope dies before it's even fully realized; Willie's court-appointed lawyers barely mounted a defense. Polly looks at the phone as it rings again, the receiver rattling in its cradle. He frowns, and brings the receiver to his ear.

"Yuh," he says. "DA Livingstone."

"Polly." He follows the voice in his mind through the long stretches of telephone wire to the kitchen on Bryant Avenue, where he can see Nell leaning against the counter, her face wearing the tight expression that's become her mask of late, impenetrable, yet somehow accusing in its impenetrability.

"Nell," he says.

"Are you coming home?"

"Yuh," he says. His eyes fall to the death warrant, which he tucks into a folder. "I had a couple of things to finish up. I'll be home soon." He glances at his wristwatch. "Sorry. I didn't realize the time."

"It's fine. Gabe's not home, yet, either. I just wasn't sure if you were coming home at all before tonight."

"No, no, I'm finished here."

There's a tap on the glass of his office door, which he'd left cracked open; he looks up as the door is pushed open the rest of the way. Earl Montgomery stands in the doorway, unshaven, burly, barrel-chested. An image of Gabe flashes into Polly's mind, of Gabe emerging terrified from the back of a car filled with other men like this one: Stout Biggs and Leroy Mason in the front seat, Pope Crowley in the back, Montgomery's heavy hand on Gabe's neck as he steered the boy from the car. That's what devastated Polly most, the man's hand on Gabe's neck, that intimate spot where his own hand falls instinctively with love.

"Well, I don't know how these things—" his wife is saying.

"Nell," Polly interrupts her. "Let me call you back."

He replaces the receiver, then turns on the desk light. He puts his hands on his desk, and stands. "Montgomery," he says.

"Evenin', prosecutor." Montgomery lifts his chin, looks at Polly down the length of his bulbous nose.

Polly waits.

"Tonight's the big night, then," Montgomery says. "You done good."

"I did my job."

Montgomery raises his eyebrows. "Some prosecute better 'n others," he says. "Never do know, what with the nigger-lovin' type. But, long as there's no last-minute hiccups, I'd say you done good."

"I did my job," Polly says again. "You can thank the jury if the sentence pleases."

Montgomery lifts his hands in a gesture of mock defense. "Nothin' intended. Just deliverin' our thanks."

Polly says nothing.

Montgomery sniffs. "And how's that boy of yours?"

Polly looks at him levelly. For a moment, he does not respond. "My boy," he says, finally, "is fine."

Gabe

The last boys get up to leave the square at once, as if on cue, getting to their feet, punching shoulders, going off home in their various directions, and soon Gabe is alone. He lies on his back in the grass, staring at the darkening sky, and when he finally decides to roll to his feet, he wonders what it is that makes him do so, right then and there. For a minute, he stands and thinks about that, but he can't pinpoint a particular motivating thought that in that instant propelled him to his feet; he simply got up, thoughtless as a hawk or darkling beetle. It makes him uneasy, to feel moved by a force that he can't identify, like a plaything being steered by an unseen giant hand.

He surveys the buildings that stand around the square: bank, city hall, post office, the building that houses the law firm of Reynolds, Browns, and Company. The buildings are lit by the square's streetlights, but their doors are shut, their windows dark, everything closed down for the weekend.

Gabe walks toward city hall, crosses the street, and wanders down the alley that runs between that building and the post office next door. The parking lot at the end of the alley, behind these buildings, is empty, but Gabe sees a square of light on the concrete, cast there by the glow of a first-story window: his father's. He is not surprised; his father has been keeping long hours, barely home before dinner's on the table, sometimes not till after. Gabe slips behind the low hedge that runs along the back of city hall. He sidesteps quietly, keeping his back to the stonework until he has reached his father's window. Then he crouches down, and slowly lifts his eyes just to the level of the sill.

Inside, his father sits at his desk, elbows on the wood and his fist against his mouth. After a moment, he straightens up, runs a hand through his hair. It is a slow, firm movement—for his father, an angry one. He drums his hand on the desktop and lifts the phone, holds the receiver between his shoulder and ear as he turns the dial; Gabe can imagine the familiar clacking sound of the disk spinning around the face. The phone is red, and one of the few items in the room that Gabe recognizes from his father's old office, in a back downstairs room at home—that and the framed chart of the Mississippi Delta hanging on the wall opposite the window. Everything else in the room—desk, bookshelf, lamp, chairs—was already there, the set and props for the person cast to play the role of DA. Gabe remembers the morning last fall when they announced his father's election, how he and his mother waited at the bottom of the stairs and clapped for his father when he came out of his bedroom, still sleepy-haired in his pajamas. Gabe wasn't sure then, is even less sure now, just what they were clapping for. It hasn't made anybody happier.

His father shifts the receiver from one ear to the other when suddenly Gabe hears sounds coming from the building's back entrance, at the top of a small stoop several yards away. He drops down into the shadows behind the hedge and presses himself against the cooling marble slabs. When he looks toward the entryway, he sees Earl Montgomery standing on the top step, framed by the wan light coming from the single bulb above the doorway. Gabe doesn't move; he scarcely dares to breathe.

He hears Montgomery sniff, then scrape a load of phlegm from his throat; when he spits, it splatters loudly on the concrete of the parking lot. The man lights a cigarette, then slowly descends the stairs. At the bottom he stops again, and draws deeply on his smoke before crossing the parking lot and disappearing into the shadows beyond. Gabe waits, unmoving. Soon he hears a car engine start, sees Montgomery's blue car driving down the street at the lot's far edge, disappearing behind the side of city hall.

Gabe watches it go. He can imagine the car's interior, the ridges in the upholstery that left marks on his bare legs, the felt material sagging from the ceiling, the empty bottles on the floor, the cross hanging from the rearview mirror, the reflection there of Montgomery's eyes, which seemed to be looking at Gabe more often than at the road. *We ain't gonna hurt you,* Montgomery said, his eyes glinting in the mirror. *Not this time. We just want to show yer daddy a lesson.* And Montgomery hadn't hurt him. None of the men had. But there he'd been, sandwiched between them for hours as they drove down country roads so dark he could see nothing but the dirt in the headlights. He'd been so scared he wet his britches, and this was the biggest shame of all, standing there as wet as a small child when they finally took him back to town.

Nell

The burned catfish she throws away, eyeing the ringing phone as she fries the next batch up, her blood churning more fiercely with each sizzling piece. Polly. She doesn't answer. The phone continues to ring, clashing with the music on the radio, which she snaps off briskly, as if it were the cause of her annoyance.

She watches the fillets cook, one at a time, the breadcrumbs crisping golden brown around the whitening meat, the oil bubbling, spattering her hands, red-hot pinpricks on her skin. She doesn't care. Her eyes water in the greasy heat. Her hair will smell of it tomorrow, even after the boy she's cooking for is gone.

Polly

There is no answer when he calls Nell back, and he sets the phone down uneasily. Montgomery's visit has made him more unsettled than he already was; he feels jittery as he locks his office for the night. His footsteps echo in the dark hallway as he walks to the back door, and the air seems to hold the memory of the barrel-chested man; his beery, foul scent lingers.

Outside, Polly pauses at the top of the stoop and gazes across the parking lot toward the tree line, where he can see the spire of St. Peter's dark against the orange sky. He imagines the courthouse nearby, where Willie Jones is in his narrow cell. Last time he saw Willie was when the sentence was read. The boy didn't flinch; he simply listened to the jury's verdict with the same bemused expression he'd maintained throughout the trial, as if he couldn't quite believe any of it. Then he'd looked at Polly and nodded, as if conceding his defeat, while in the third row his mother began to weep.

Next time he sees Willie Jones, the boy'll be strapped in the chair.

Polly rubs his eyes, and he's just started down the stairs when he hears a rustle in the bushes along the building to his left. He wheels around, expecting Montgomery again, or Stout Biggs or Leroy or Pope, but it's Gabe he sees rising from the shrubbery. At the sight of his son, he feels a wave of primal anger start to gather itself deep within him. "I swear to God, if that man . . ." he begins.

"I'm OK," Gabe says. "I was waiting for you."

"Then Montgomery . . ."

"He didn't see me."

"He didn't bring you here."

"No, I told you. I was just waiting for you."

Polly runs a hand through his hair. Used to be, when he was first DA, that Gabe would wait for him all the time; only now does Polly realize it's been months since they've walked home together. He wonders if it's because Gabe is frightened by what happened with Montgomery or if it's because he himself has been so preoccupied with other things, with Willie Jones. "Come on out of the bushes, son," he says.

They walk home quietly through the heat, kicking an acorn back and forth, taking turns. Polly asks Gabe about his day, about his math test, about his baseball game, but tonight the boy doesn't seem much for talking, and Polly doesn't push him. He watches their shadows, which grow as they pass through the glow of different streetlights from dark pools beneath their feet to long, thin strips across the pavement, then disappear altogether in the darkness between pockets of light. One tall, one half-size, any father and son.

"Dad," Gabe says finally, in the quiet. He kicks the acorn, which skitters several yards down the street; it has traveled with them all this way, from the squares of downtown New Iberia to the tree-lined streets of the neighborhood where they live.

"Yes, Gabe."

"You sure Willie Jones is guilty?"

They have come to the acorn; Polly kicks it before answering, and glances at his son; this is the line of questioning he'd been waiting for. "What makes you ask, son?"

"Caliber said some folks in St. Martinville say it wasn't rape at all."

"That so."

"Yessir."

"What do they say it was?"

Gabe shrugs, kicks the acorn.

"Well," Polly says, "folks will say what they will. But I do believe that Willie Jones is guilty."

"Otherwise you wouldn't have persecuted him?"

"Prosecuted. That's right. Otherwise I wouldn't have taken the case."

The acorn has come to rest at the edge of the sidewalk; Polly steps toward it, kicks it back to center. "What else did Caliber say?" he asks, warily.

"That the chair's name is Gruesome Gertie."

Polly does not reply.

Gabe kicks the acorn. "Does it hurt?"

"Does what hurt?" He knows what Gabe is asking about, and he knows the answer; he's seen it once before, as an official witness to the last execution in the parish some eleven years ago. He remembers vividly the jolt of the body, the quivering limbs, the spread of goose pimples across smooth flesh. The image has haunted him since, and he dreads tonight, having to see it again, this time with the knowledge that he is responsible.

"The chair."

Polly kicks the acorn. "It's quick. Too quick to hurt."

"Buddy Cunningham's father is taking him to see it."

"Is that so."

"That's what Buddy said."

"Well, the Cunninghams will do as the Cunninghams do. And they may well be disappointed because there won't be much to see."

Gabe seems to hesitate, and then: "Can I go with you?"

Polly glances quickly at his son. "Certainly not. I have no choice but to go. Believe me, I wouldn't otherwise." He looks at his son again, and frowns. "Why would you want to go?"

Gabe shrugs. "When you were twelve your father took you to see the black folks strung up in the tree," he reasons. "You showed me the picture."

"Yes," Polly concedes. "He did. And I hated it." He pauses, ruminating. "But you know," he says, "I think it's partly the reason I chose to become a lawyer."

Gabe looks at him, confused. "Why?"

"Well, legal justice is important. Lawyers, trials, juries, all that. Think about what happens otherwise, when folks take matters into their own hands. Those men in the picture ended up in the tree. And think of last year. Moses Beauparlant ended up in the kilns and Frix Mobley in the salt mines. What kind of justice is that?"

Gabe pauses in front of the acorn, seems to consider it as he considers Polly's words. Then he looks up. "But Willie's case . . ." he begins. "That was legal justice. And I don't really see why the chair is any better."

Father Hannigan

T he streetlights have come on for the evening by the time
Hannigan reaches Bryant Avenue, a street lined by col-
orfully shingled Victorian homes whose details—the dentils
in the molding, the lattice of the front porches, the elegant
entablature—make Hannigan think of snowflakes. He peers
into the shadows of each portico to read the numbers hanging above the front door. When he finds number twenty-five,
he stops and rests his hands on the still-warm metal of the
low iron gate.

Twenty-five is set back farther from the street than most
of the houses on Bryant Avenue, beyond a well-tended garden,
lush despite the dry weather. The windows at the front of the
house are dark, but through one Hannigan can see the glow
from a lit room somewhere in the back. He opens the gate,
latches it quietly behind him. Instead of climbing the stairs
to the front porch, he follows a small path that leads around
the side of the house, as he has been instructed to do.

He comes around the house and sees, across a mossy
patio, the kitchen, a square room off the back of the building. The door is open, and warm yellow light spills from the
kitchen into the night, illuminating a green pocket of shrubbery, moss, stone, and grass. Bugs flit against the screen,
through which Hannigan can see the woman from yesterday
bent over a counter, her hands moving rapidly before her.

For a moment, he stands in the shadows and observes her, the air heavy with the scent of butterfly ginger, the white blossoms around him like so many fragile wings. Her hands are winglike, too, quick and darting as she wraps food with crinkling foil, spreads a cloth over a basket, cuts a length of string. When she has finished, she sets her hands down on the counter, and lowers her head.

Hannigan steps out of the shadows and crosses the patio toward the kitchen door. He taps against the screen; the woman lifts her head and hurries to the door. "Father," she says, through the mesh. Her face has the same determined expression that it had when she approached him outside the courthouse yesterday. He had never seen her before, but she was somehow deeply familiar to him, in a way that made him feel both uneasy and compelled. She needed to see Willie, she said. She didn't say why, and he didn't ask.

"I've wrapped up his supper," she says now, going back to the counter for the basket, which she carries to the door in the crook of her arm. Behind her, Hannigan can see an old woman sitting at the kitchen table, silent and unmoving. "Catfish, potatoes, and pecan pie like he asked for. And green beans, even though he didn't. I tried my hand at collards, but they weren't fit to eat. Not for a last meal, anyway."

"It's good of you." He looks at her through the screen, hesitates. Then, "I realize I don't even know your name," he says.

"It's Nell." She opens the door and steps down onto the patio, and for a moment, she simply stands there, gazing into the middle distance. "I'm not religious," she says, finally, and

Hannigan isn't sure if this is an apology or a confession. Nell looks at him. "I'm not sure I believe in God."

Hannigan regards her, says nothing, though he thinks he could say the same. Her eyes are dark and glinting.

"And I don't know if he's guilty or not," she continues, "but either way I don't think a boy oughta be put to death."

Nell looks at him searchingly, and he wonders what she's looking for. For wisdom, maybe, in the vessel of a priest.

"Do you?" she asks.

"That's not for me to judge. My duty is to offer guidance and love. That's all."

"You may be a priest, but that doesn't mean you don't hold opinions. Does it bother you, what's happening tonight?"

Hannigan doesn't answer right away. His mind skitters, a thousand frantic thoughts at once that make him want to weep. "Yes," he manages to say.

And then there is only the hush of the garden, the ribbit of a frog.

Nell's gaze is steady, her expression both dismayed and resigned. She holds the basket out; he takes it from her.

"Well," she says. "Then there it is." He doesn't know if she means the dinner or something else.

Nell

Wordlessly, the priest turns and disappears into the shadows of the garden. Nell sinks onto the single step outside the kitchen door. She has not slept well in days, less and less each night, lying awake in wait for Polly to come finally to bed, lying sleepless still even after the mattress has sunk beneath his weight and his breathing has turned into a fretful snore.

She rests her elbows on her knees, lowers her head into her palms, and stares down at the stone beneath her bare feet. Several inches away, she sees a line of tiny ants parading by. She puts her toe into their path; the first ant pauses, then goes around it, and continues on in its original direction. The others follow. When she moves her toe away, it's as if it's there yet, the line of ants curving still around the memory of where it used to be.

She lifts her head and settles her chin into her hand. She can smell grease on her fingertips, and hopes the catfish will still be warm by the time it reaches the boy. She packed up enough for the priest to have some, too, and regrets forgetting to tell him so. It was a sad thing to imagine the boy having to eat his last supper alone. She'd already left the fishmonger when she thought of it, then had to go back for more. The women in line behind her were talking about the boy, how it was sad that even the young ones couldn't keep their trousers zipped. She'd stared hard at the glassy round eye of a snapper on ice.

Behind her, a moth thumps madly against the screen, and when she reaches out to brush the moth away, she is surprised by the power of its beating wings against her palm, less butterfly than beast, a ball of flapping fury that turns into dust against her hand.

Lane

Taverns and saloons sit along the banks of Bayou Teche, where it runs parallel to Main Street, the reflections of their lights murky smudges on the brown water. The faint sounds of jazz and Cajun music murmur in the air as Seward and Lane walk from the truck to the door of Lou's Tavern, where Seward promises the steak is fine. They leave the truck on Fulton Street, where it sits parked beneath a streetlamp, looking as ordinary as any other truck but for the extra muffler and the exhaust pipe rising from the roof.

Lane keeps his head low, eyes fixed on his own feet as they pass over the ground: concrete, cobblestone, and curb. The warden gave him shoes this morning, a pair of brown street loafers to replace the work boots he wears in the fields all day, and their unfamiliarity gives him the sense that he's being transported by a body not his own. These are a version of the shoes they'd given him to wear the only other time he'd been let out, to attend his mother's funeral; he remembers the smooth prints they left in the graveside dirt where he stood handcuffed, a prison guard by his side. Why the shoes, he doesn't know; that first time, for the funeral, he wore the same T-shirt and denim he wears inside every day, and he does so again now.

The tavern is a single-story wooden building with a low aluminum-covered porch in front. Though it's still early, the place is crowded inside, Friday night. The stools along the bar are taken and the dance floor is full, everyone waltzing to "Jolie Blonde," played by one man with a fiddle and another with a squeeze-box over in the corner of the room. Seward and Lane sit down at one of the few empty tables, by a window overlooking the Teche.

Seward taps his fingers on the table in time to the music, hums along. "You know this song?" he asks.

"I think I might've heard it."

"Written by an inmate at Port Arthur." Seward raises his eyebrows. "You know that?"

Lane shakes his head.

"But I reckon when you're in prison you've got that sort a time on your hands."

Lane looks at the captain levelly. Seward has been drinking steadily from his flask since they arrived in New Iberia. He's said more in the past hour than he has over the course of the afternoon, and Lane isn't sure if he doesn't prefer silence.

"I reckon." He lets his eyes drift from the captain to the room beyond, to the dance floor. Faces come into and go out of focus, drunk, smiling, grotesque, and then one is coming closer, young, pretty, the white face of a girl. Lane lowers his eyes, as if that would make her stop, as if his gaze were reeling her in.

It is the waitress; he understands this when he sees a smooth hand slide a dish of peanuts onto the table, and an empty bowl for the shells. Her shoes are loafers, sensible. Her stocking has a run that disappears beneath the hem of her dress, and its suggested trajectory causes something inside him to tighten abruptly. "Evenin', y'all," she says.

Lane looks up. The girl's features are as delicate as her voice; her hair is dark around a narrow face. Her eyes are dark, too, so dark Lane can't tell where iris ends and pupil begins. She wears a checked dress with a white collar beneath her apron, and heavy makeup, though Lane thinks she can't be much more than a girl.

Seward shifts his whole body in his seat to look up at her. "Thank you, baby doll," he says.

"What can I get y'all?"

Seward pats the table. "Two whiskeys, two steaks. I like mine bloody." He looks at Lane. "You?"

"Just regular. No whiskey."

Seward reaches for the girl's hand before she can turn to go. "Two whiskeys, two steaks," he repeats.

The girl glances at Lane uncertainly, then nods.

Seward turns in his seat to watch her walk away across the room. Then he settles back into his chair with a comfortable sigh, and studies Lane. "So you the teetotaling type?"

"Not mostly."

"Just every now and then."

Lane shrugs. "Don't seem right in the circumstance."

"You don't drink, I'll drink it for you." The captain slaps his thigh. "This here leg's hollow."

Lane lifts a peanut from the dish, squeezes the shell between his fingers. It's cardboard soft, wrong for a nut that isn't boiled, and he sets it down on the table.

"That's a nice-looking scar," Seward says. He's looking at Lane's hand, at the line that runs across the knuckles.

Lane traces the scar with his fingertips. "I reckon it oughta been stitched."

Seward sniffs. "What you in for anyway?"

"You know what I'm in for."

"Burglary. Murder." Seward raises his hands. "Dime a dozen. What's your *story*, boy?"

"Ain't got one."

"Bullshit. Why'd you do it?"

The girl returns with their whiskeys, and Seward takes a long sip of his. Lane looks down at his own drink; the ice cubes gleam in the amber liquid, and condensation beads on the glass. He doesn't drink.

He looks at the captain. "I didn't plan to kill the man. I was burgling his home."

"Didn't answer why."

"You need money, you need money."

The captain drinks some more, as if to quench his thirst. He grimaces, sets his glass down. "You need money, you work."

"Sometimes," Lane says, "working ain't enough."

Seward plucks a peanut from the bowl, tears open the shell with his teeth. For a moment, he just looks at Lane, slowly chewing his peanut. Then he throws back the rest of his drink, and Lane can see through the bottom of the glass the man's crooked yellow teeth, his fat tongue. He puts his glass down and pushes back from the table. "Gotta take a piss," he says.

Lane watches him limp across the room, one-two, one-two, one-two, his own father's gait after he'd got caught up in the harvester. Lane remembers his shouts from the cane field, and trying to follow the sound through the soft muck soil among the stalks, the cane leaves slashing at his skin.

Working wasn't enough after that. One-two, one-two, one-two, his father's drunken footsteps across the midnight floor.

The captain disappears in the crowd, and Lane turns toward the window and presses his head against the glass. Outside on the bayou, a man drifts by in a canoe, using his paddle only to steer. He vanishes into the tendrils of a willow tree hanging low over the surface of the water. Lane wishes he could vanish, too. He thinks of the crossroads earlier, how the roads stretched off in all directions, how if he ran he could have gone anywhere, yet how for him there wasn't anywhere to go.

Ora

They keep hogs and chickens out behind the station, the chickens in a coop of metal mesh and plywood, the hogs in a pen of woven wire affixed to wooden fence posts, with an aluminum lean-to over one end to give the creatures shelter. There are three hogs, twelve chickens. There were thirteen until last week. Ora doesn't know what happened to the last, but she can guess. There were no feathers involved, there was no suggestion of violence. She's said nothing about it to Dale, figures: what's a chicken? Figures he might not see it that way.

Ora feeds these animals twice a day: once at sunup, before the Mayes boy has left for the day and Ora's shift in the store has started; and once again just after sundown, once he's returned for his night shift at the pump. She stands in the deepening dark tossing handfuls of chicken feed and watching as the birds peck halfheartedly, bluck-blucking their grumbling distaste. They're holding out for the contents of the bucket hung from the crook of her elbow, the kitchen bucket, which tonight she's filled with too-hard raisins, eggplant leaves, potato skins, and carrot peels—the sort of leavings she used to bring for the pigs, the good stuff. When she finally obliges them and scatters the kitchen scraps, the birds burst into excited squawkery. They dart and peck and fight over these delicacies as if they hadn't just had feed, more appreciative of slop than the pigs ever were. Ora looks over at the pigs now, lazing in post-meal stupor. They are fat, these hogs, pink and brown tubs of creatures happy with soybean meal and whey. It's no wonder the last one's taken so long to eat.

Not far from the chicken coop and hogpen is an old shed, a relic from some former time where they keep spare wire, pellets, straw bales for bedding, muck shovels, and chicken feed. Ora brings the empty buckets inside here and hangs them on the nail hooks along the far wall. Along the other wall, beneath the shed's single window, is an old pine bench where Ora takes herself to sit sometimes. The initials *A. T. V.* are carved into the bench seat, and the date *1854.* The bench reminds her of a time both different and the same, of Tobe as a sleepless babe, how she'd walk with him up and down, up and down the edge of the field, how when she'd lulled him finally to sleep, instead of going back inside the station, she'd take him there, to that bench inside the shed, and there he'd sleep, and she could sit, thoughtless and still, and stare out over the fields.

They didn't keep hogs or chickens then; the meat they ate was part of that delivered frozen in bulk to the store, the eggs came from the cartons delivered with the dairy. Though she had little experience, the live animals were her idea. She thought it would be good for the boy, and, for a time, Tobe did seem to enjoy tossing the chickens their feed or watching the hogs wallow in the short-lived mud pits she'd make by pouring water into shallow indentations in the dirt. Aside from transporting hogs down to New Iberia for slaughter when it was time, Dale had little to do with the project, still doesn't, but Ora doesn't mind.

After she has hung up the buckets and refastened the bags of feed, Ora stands in the shed doorway and looks back at the station. The bedroom and kitchen windows are dark, but she can imagine the building's other side, and knows that by now it is aglow, the store's fluorescent light spilling from the windows. She hears the sound of an engine, and when she looks eastward down the highway she sees a truck approaching, a dark square shape against the blueing sky. The driver snaps the headlights on as he nears the lonely crossroads, as if reminded only by the station's lights that it is now that time. He doesn't stop.

Ora stands in the doorway and listens to the noise of the truck fade, and in the silence that ensues she has the impression that she is not alone. She cocks her head, listening closely, and sure enough, she soon hears a rustle of movement through the cotton, gentle whispering voices from among the bolls. She knows that whoever is approaching cannot see her where she's standing in the shed doorway. The rustling grows louder, then stops. Ora frowns. At the edge of the field, a voice begins to whisper, but it is quickly hushed by another, and then there is a sneeze. Ora feels her shoulders soften: the sneeze of a child.

She steps out through the doorway, reveals herself. The boy from earlier is standing at the edge of the field with another, smaller boy. She is surprised by the rush of pleasure she feels; it is akin to the thrill of a forbidden courtship.

When the boys see Ora, the smaller one turns and starts to run.

"Hey!" she calls. "It's all right!"

The first boy hasn't moved. He eyes her as she walks from the shed to the edge of the field. The smaller boy hangs back, several feet into the cotton, but he has stopped running.

"What y'all up to?" she says.

The boys say nothing.

"Let me guess," she says. She stops at the edge of the field, about where she stood earlier, and puts her hands on her hips. "Y'all are back for more candy."

"See!" the first boy exclaims, calling over his shoulder to the smaller boy. "I tole you she give me them caramels!" He turns back to Ora. "He dint believe me," he says, indignantly. "He dint believe you even talked to me. His momma tole him you devilin' folks."

For a minute, Ora is quiet, letting this sink in. "That so," she says, finally.

The boy just looks at her.

Ora shifts her weight from one foot to the other. "Tell you what," she says. "Y'all wait here. Got no more caramels inside, but I'll see if I can't find somethin' better."

Dale

In the store, Dale can hear her footsteps in the kitchen, the sticky sound of bare feet on linoleum. He looks up from the newspaper he'd spread open on the counter, listens to her take the lid off the pot on the stove, hears the tap, tap, tap of the spoon against the edge of the pot after she's stirred what's inside. He hears her open one cabinet, then another, hears the rustling of cellophane. He listens to his wife in anticipation, expecting her to enter the store, but she does not come in, leaving him both unsettled and at the same time relieved. He hears the kitchen door close gently as she goes back outside, and then it is quiet.

He leaves his post behind the counter and walks over to the shop door. Across the lot, the light above the pump is flickering, has been for the past few nights, Dale can't figure why. Beyond, Benny Mayes sits with a sandwich in the cab of his pickup, the overhead light on, waiting for the rare customer who comes for gas by night.

Dale opens the door and steps out. The dog, pressed up against the concrete storefront, eyes Dale without lifting his head, his tail thumping the ground, tentative and weary. Hot. Dale can't blame him. He squats down to touch the dirt, and it is warm beneath his hand. He refills the dish that Ora has put out for the dog with water from the spigot, and the dog scrambles to his feet and drinks thirstily; Dale listens to the sound as he walks away, drawing closer to Benny's truck, where Bing Crosby croons on the radio.

Benny doesn't seem to notice Dale approaching, he's so intent on his sandwich, a big meaty thing dripping with mayonnaise. Dale taps his fingers on the door frame, and Benny looks at him through the open window with surprise, his mouth full.

"Fine-lookin' sandwich," Dale says. Benny holds the thing out, offering, chewing. Dale shakes his head. "Mind if I sit?"

Benny waves his hand, *come in*, and Dale walks around to the passenger side. Benny turns down the radio as he climbs in. "Sure you don't want any? I got more than I need," he says, offering his sandwich again. "Ma sent me with two."

"Nah. Ora got some stew on. Reckon she'll want to eat once she's done out back." He sniffs, rubs at his nose, watches a pair of headlights slow as they come to the crossroads, then carry on past.

"I notice them lights been flickering," Benny says, nodding toward the light above the pumps.

"Yuh. Checked the bulb, but it's tight."

"Reckon it could be the heat?"

Dale lifts his hand from where it rests on the door frame; he doesn't know.

"I had enough of this heat myself," Benny says, after a minute.

"Mmmhmmm."

On the radio, Bing Crosby has stopped his singing, and a man's voice talks excitedly about Beech-Nut gum. *Can't beat it for quality and refreshment!*

"You heard from Tobe?" Benny asks, glancing over at Dale.

Dale brings his hand to his mouth, strokes his chin. Then he reaches into his pocket for the folded letter he's been carrying there all week, hands it over for Benny to read. He realizes his hands are trembling.

Benny opens the letter, stares at it for some time. He opens his mouth, as if to speak, but says nothing. He looks at Dale, then looks at the letter again. "Dale," he says.

"Came last week." Dale rubs his eyes. "I thought they were supposed to come and tell you. Not just send that kind of news in the mail."

Benny looks at him. "How's Ora?"

Dale shakes his head. "I haven't told her," he says. "I can't. I can't bring myself to do it." He shuts his eyes and covers them with a hand. "Just keep on kind of hoping that they'll come." He shakes his head again. "'Cause I don't know if I can be the one."

Ora

They are waiting for her out behind the shed, side by side on the ground, their backs to the wall and their skinny bare legs outstretched. They look up at her, their eyes four white saucers in the light of the rising moon.

Ora squats down before them, opens her hand. On her palm rest two orange-brown candies wrapped in crisp clear paper. The boys look at the candies, and then at Ora, skeptical, uncertain.

"Chicken Bones," she says. She thrusts her hand forward. "Go on, try them."

The first boy takes a candy, looks at it, smells it.

"Well, go on, unwrap it. You can't rightly smell it through the cellophane," Ora urges.

The boy untwists the wrapper, holds the candy pinched between his fingers, as if it were some biting critter.

"Well, it's not gonna hurt you!" Ora laughs. "You like peanut butter?"

The boy nods.

"And you like coconut?"

The boy shrugs. "Ain't had it."

"It's good. And this here's just a whole bunch of peanut butter all rolled up with coconut."

The boy examines the candy. "Ain't a bone, then?" he asks.

"A bone!" Ora laughs again. "No wonder you didn't want to eat it! No, that's just what they're called. Chicken Bones. Looks kind of like a bone, right? But not a bit of bone in there. Just peanut and coconut, like I said."

The boy puts it into his mouth and chews.

"Good?"

He nods. "Crunchy," he says, through his mouthful.

Ora extends her palm to the other boy, the smaller one, who takes the remaining piece of candy from her with the furtive quickness of a squirrel. He opens it rapidly and puts it into his mouth, watching Ora nervously all the while.

"Good, right?" she asks him.

He nods, his eyes wide as he chews.

"That's even better than that caramel thing," the first boy says. "That's good!"

Ora nods. "Thought y'all would like them," she says. "They're my boy's favorite, too."

The first boy looks both curious and surprised. "You got a boy in there?" he asks, gesturing toward the station.

Ora shakes her head. "Nah, not in there," she says, and she can feel her smile fading. She looks off across the field for a moment, then returns her gaze to the boy. "My boy's gone off to the war," she says.

The boy looks at her solemnly. "Ain't a boy, then," he says. "Not like me."

"Not like you," Ora agrees. "But still a boy to me." She rests her elbows on her knees, squatting before them. "Your mamas know where y'all are?" she asks.

The boys glance at each other.

"I'm guessing that means no."

The smaller boy pulls his knees in to his chest, looks at the ground. The older boy looks Ora in the eye. "No ma'am," he admits. "Reckon they don't."

Ora's knees pop as she stands. "Look," she says. "Seems to me y'all best get home before it's full dark, you hear?"

"Yes ma'am." The older boy gets to his feet, reaches down, and pulls the smaller boy up. He looks at Ora impishly, emboldened. "You got any more those chicken candies?"

Ora puts her hands on her hips. "Well, now," she says. "Just maybe I do. But look," she says, reaching into her pocket for two more of the candies. "Too much candy in a day's bad for your teeth. Rot right out of your head. I'll send you each home with another, but you got to promise to save it for tomorrow." She looks from one boy to the other, back and forth. "Promise?"

They nod.

She puts one candy into each boy's hand. "Let me ask y'all something before you go."

They look up at her expectantly, waiting, but it's too much to put into words, the thing she wants to ask. "Never mind," she says. "I just hope we can be friends. That y'all won't stay away."

And though they nod before they go, once they've vanished in the dimming rows of cotton, Ora feels more alone than ever.

Dale

Ora is still out with the animals when Dale comes back into the station. He walks through the store to the kitchen, where he guesses he'll find supper on the table, Ora waiting. But the kitchen is empty, the table bare. He surveys the kitchen with bemusement. When he looks toward the window above the sink for signs of Ora in the yard, he finds it's grown dark enough outside that in the glass he can see nothing but his own blurred reflection: a man standing alone in a room.

He crosses the kitchen to the screen door, calls through it. "Ora?"

He listens: bugs, katydids. He looks up, finds the face in the risen moon.

"Ore?"

His voice doesn't echo; the fields swallow the sound.

He frowns, pushing open the door, and he's about to step outside to look for his wife when he notices her shadow, cast by moonlight on the other side of the shed. She's leaning up against the building, he can tell by her slanting shadow, and he can tell by her silence that she wants not to be found.

Quietly, he lets the door close and turns into the kitchen. His back is tired and the chair beckons, but he doesn't want to sit down, doesn't want to think. Instead, he crosses to the stove, where the burner is on beneath the stew. He stirs the bubbling liquid, as he imagines Ora would do, and then he starts to set the table: straw placemats, white china plates yellowing with age, plastic cups cloudy with scratch marks. He folds the paper napkins carefully, can't remember where the fork goes, on the left or on the right, can't remember which goes inside, spoon or knife. He stirs the stew. He puts bowls atop the plates, in case that's what she intended, and fills their cups with cold water from the jug. He moves the forks to the other side, but it looks wrong, and he moves them back again. He stirs the stew. He sees corn bread on the counter, so decides to take the bowls away, and then he hears Ora in the doorway.

"You can leave those," she says.

He turns, a bowl in either hand. Ora is leaning against the door frame, watching him, and from her posture it seems that she has been watching for some time.

"Turned out soupier than I intended," she says. "Bowls'll be better." She straightens up and takes the bowls from his hand, puts a hunk of corn bread in each, and then ladles atop the corn bread steaming spoonfuls of stew. She sets the bowls on the table, then gets a salad of cucumber and radish from the fridge. Dale stands just where he was when she came in, watching her, so near, yet so distant, her heart half a world away. Dale wants her back the way she wants Tobe, and he fears that to show her the letter would be to lose them both.

"Well, go on now, sit," she says, meeting his gaze as she squeezes a lime over the vegetables. "What are you standing there for?"

Dale obeys. "Smells good," he says, spooning up a bite, which he lets cool for a moment before putting it in his mouth.

"Should be all right." Ora sits down, shifting her place setting so that it is not directly across from him, and a third spot glares.

For a few moments, they eat in silence. Dale tries to think of conversation, but his mind keeps coming back to the letter in his pocket. He looks at Ora across the table, and his heart starts to race.

He clears his throat. "Everything OK out there, with the animals?"

"Just fine. Got more eggs than I can do with."

"Can send some home with Benny. He brought some figs. I set 'em on the counter," Dale says, gesturing.

Ora nods. "I'll pack some up," she says. And then they are quiet again. Their spoons click and scrape in the silence.

"Benny said ol' Art's gone to see the execution," Dale says, after a minute.

Ora looks up questioningly, her spoon full.

"Execution over in St. Martinville," Dale says. "Been in the paper. Thought you'd a heard."

Ora shakes her head.

"They brung the chair down from Angola."

"Execution for what?" Ora asks, spoon still in midair.

Dale shrugs, scrapes up his last bit of stew. "Some damn nigger raped a girl, some such," he says. He puts the bite into his mouth.

Ora's eyes harden, and she sets her spoon down. "Wish you wouldn't use that word."

"I'll say nigger if he acts like one, raping a girl like that." He swallows his mouthful.

"And what if it was a white man did the raping?" Ora asks. "What would you call him, then?" she demands, and in the singular inquisitive expression on her face Dale so clearly sees their son that the hard truth of the letter he's been hiding hits him like a kick in the gut.

His eyes flicker and dart around the room. He pushes back from the table and brings his bowl to the stove, and he stands there and he fills it, and he fills it because though he isn't hungry, he cannot let Ora see him fighting not to cry.

Frank

The cotton is waist high around him, ripe with brimming bolls, which seem in the dim light a single substance blanketing the field, like how Frank imagines snow. The dry bracts scrape against his trousers, a swishing sound with each step, and his feet sink into the loose-tilled soil, so that walking takes twice the effort it would need otherwise. Frank finds he has to pause every few minutes to catch his breath. He keeps his eyes fixed on the cabin in the distance, still just a small shape beneath the rising moon. Smoke drifts from the chimney. It doesn't seem to be getting any bigger, as if Frank were making no progress toward it at all. But when he looks back in the direction from which he's come, Bess is growing ever smaller, a tiny shape alone with the wagon and stone at the edge of the empty road. He feels as if he's wading into nothingness, a purgatory of perpetual cotton.

It's grown no cooler with evening, the heat now rising from the ground, enveloping, escapeless. He left his jacket in the wagon, but he's still in long white shirtsleeves and brown wool pants, hardly summertime clothing, but his finest. In his estimation eighty-five dollars was too much to ask to borrow in a pair of coveralls. He stops to take his loosened tie from around his neck, remembering this morning, when Elma tied it on, and his heart seizes at the memory. He thinks how Elma could soon be all that he has left.

He continues on, trying not to think of the miles between where he is and where he needs to be, of the shrinking
hours between now and midnight. Images flash through his
mind: Elma's gnarled hand around the rocker's arm, the ex-
plosions and gunsmoke of war, the tombstone in the wagon
bed, the banker's mocking face, scattered hay and stockings
in the shed. He stares at the white blur of cotton as he trudges
through it, trying to see this instead, until finally he has come
to the clearing where the cabin stands.

He looks up, breathless and sweating, the tie still
clenched firmly in his hand. The cabin is even smaller than
it appeared from afar, rickety and raised above the ground on
cinder blocks. Laundry hangs from a line in the small yard:
trousers, a blouse, white undershirts glowing in the moonlight. Three sagging steps lead up to a deep sunporch, where
a rake leans against the rough-cut cypress boards of the wall.
There are no outbuildings, like the one where he keeps Bess,
and there is no sign of a mule.

A dog comes out through the open door. It walks to the
edge of the porch, where it growls, a low, guttural sound. A
child follows. Frank stands in the moonlight at the edge of the
clearing, what hope he had for help now gone. A cacophony
of locusts swells around him, jeering and shrill, and he feels
suddenly exhausted, the weight of the day, of the year, of his
life crashing into him from behind. It is all he can do to lift
his hand. The child lifts her own, and, like that, it is dark.

Willie

It is dark outside when Willie hears the familiar tenor of Father Hannigan's voice coming from somewhere down the hallway. He sits up. The sound of the priest's voice fills him with the same warm relief he remembers feeling in the dark hours as a child when finally he heard the latching of the front door and the footsteps on the floorboards that told him that his father had come home. His father. Willie's throat tightens at the thought. Their last embrace was the first of the lasts, and so far has been the worst. He looks toward the spot where they stood, holding each other. Father Hannigan had led his mother away; even so, Willie could hear her sobbing somewhere down the hallway, a terrible sound. He had kept his eyes open and fixed on a crack in the paint of the wall, as if staring at this would somehow keep him grounded, in control, the only bulwark against the sense he felt of grief and regret and longing so eviscerating that it threatened to break him down completely.

He takes a shaky breath and looks toward the cell door, waiting, listening to the murmur of their conversation crystallize into words as the sheriff and the priest approach. The two have been his most frequent visitors in the past eight months, though it is rare that Willie sees them together. Grazer he sees three or four brief times a day: once at each meal and occasionally once in between—a delivery of mail, a candy bar, and now and again, for no real reason at all, he'll just appear, drape his armpits over the mid-rail, and drawl. Father Hannigan Willie sees once a week. He comes, and sometimes they talk, but mostly they spend the time playing the card games that the priest has taught him: gin rummy, piquet, cribbage, marjolet. It is the one time when Willie can forget everything that's happening.

The sheriff swings the door open, but instead of gesturing the priest into the cell or stepping inside himself, he puts his hands on his hips and regards Willie from where he stands between the bars. "Well, bald Willie," he says. "The good father brung you a final supper and reckons you ought to eat it proper."

Willie looks from the sheriff to the priest behind him. Father Hannigan smiles at him and nods. "Good evening, Willie."

Willie gives a single nod. His last supper, he thinks. His last embrace, his last sunset, and now his last supper.

"Well, come on, boy," the sheriff says. "Up and at 'em. Let's go, go, go!" He gestures Willie up from the cot with an impatient wave of his hand.

Willie follows the men back down the hallway. The three pass the doors of the other seven cells, all of them empty save Burl's and that of one other man, who lies facedown on his cot, head in the crook of his elbow. This is the man Willie heard weeping earlier, but he doesn't know his name, or what he's in for. Burl is standing at his cell door, gripping the bars; Willie nods to him as they pass, and Burl nods in return.

At the end of the corridor, they pause as the sheriff opens a hand-cranked row of bars. On the other side is the bullpen,

THE MERCY SEAT

where normally deputies and guards gather to listen to the radio or play bourré; Willie can hear them from his cell. He's passed through the room before, on his way to or from the courthouse during his trial. Tonight the room is empty. On the table where Willie has seen coffee mugs and playing cards is a large wicker basket. The room smells not of cigarettes and coffee, but of garlic, rosemary, grease. It smells like home. Hannigan goes to the table and pulls out a chair. "Sit, Willie," he says. Willie sits, and Hannigan slides the basket in front of him. "Your supper."

Lane

"Both look bloody, I'm afraid." The waitress stands above Lane in her checked dress, a plate in either hand. She sets one down in front of Seward's empty seat, the other in front of Lane. "That gonna be all right for you?"

He looks at the meat, pink flesh and gristle. "That's just fine," he says. He nods, waits for the girl to go away. She waits, too, expectant, her hands clasped behind her back, and Lane feels suddenly uncomfortable.

"You from around here?" she asks him.

"No, we ain't."

"Y'all just passing through?"

"So to speak."

The girl shifts her weight from one foot to the other. "Where y'all headed next?"

"Back where we come from."

"Where's that?"

Lane regards the girl. Even with all the makeup she wears, she looks innocent, the kind of girl that sleeps beneath one of those lacy white canopies he's seen in the upstairs bedroom of a stranger's house, a doll and a teddy bear on the white armchair in the corner. "You sure ask a lot of questions," he says.

"And you sure don't seem to like to answer." She smiles at him coyly, her fingers landing briefly on Lane's shoulder.

He flinches involuntarily; he cannot remember the last time a woman touched him.

"No," he says shortly, more brusquely than he means to. He looks at her. "Don't reckon I do."

The girl's smile fades, and even in the room's dim light Lane can see the blush sweep across her face. He feels weary, and rubs his eyes with one hand. "It ain't you," he means to say next, but when he drops his hand and looks up for the girl, she's gone, and he sees the captain returning to the table, where the steaks marinate in their own red juices.

Frank

When Frank opens his eyes, he finds himself in a rocking chair by a fire. Three small children sit near his feet, staring up at him curiously from the wooden floorboards. A man stands by the hearth, one elbow on the mantel. His other hand rests on the shoulder of a boy, maybe nine or ten years old. Their eyes are upon him, too. A woman paces in the shadows beyond, humming softly to the baby in her arms. Her humming is the only sound aside from the crackle of the fire, and then footsteps: a girl approaches with a cup of water, drawn from the wooden bucket in the corner of the room. She gives it to him shyly, all ebony skin and bone in a ragged white dress.

"Thank you," Frank says. He takes the offered cup, his hands trembling, and drinks it at once. The water is warm and earthy; he closes his eyes and imagines he can feel it flowing through his veins. He lowers the cup and wipes his mouth.

"You hungry?" the man asks, from the mantel. He is tall, thin like his daughter, in a dirty white shirt and trousers held up by suspenders. He gestures toward the pot hanging over the hearth. "Got stew left."

Frank shakes his head, though he hasn't eaten since morning. "Be obliged for more water, though," he says.

The girl glances at her father, who nods. She takes the cup from Frank and returns to the bucket, where she ladles the last of the water up. The man taps the shoulder of the boy beside him, who goes to the bucket and takes it with him out through the back door.

Frank nods his thanks to the girl and drinks again, this time slowly, sip by sip, each sip restoring him further, bringing the room into clearer focus. It is the cabin's only room, with a front and back door, glassless windows. There are two ladder-back chairs at a wooden table, and a freestanding cabinet where the family keeps cups and plates. On the other side of the room are two mattresses. These are dirty and bare. The walls are also bare, the plaster falling off in many places. Frank grew up in a cabin like this one, lived in one till he got the sugar job and moved near to town with Elma. But he knows this life. It had been a source of pride for him to be able to give his children more, some schooling, bedsheets, better clothes, though lately he's wondered what good it did.

"What's your business here?" the man asks.

In the mother's arms, the baby begins to whimper, and the mother starts to sing softly, a tune Frank doesn't recognize. He looks at her, pacing in the dim light, then turns to the man. "I'se on my way to St. Martinville. Mule won't budge. Left her out on the road edge. Hoped y'all'd have one could pull my load the last miles."

The man makes a noise with his throat, a scoffing sound. "No sah, no mule here."

"I seen that."

"Mule hurt?"

Frank shakes his head. "Old. Been from St. Martinville to Youngsville and back. Or just about. Ain't used to more than a half mile these days."

"You can shelter here the night," the man says.

"No sah," Frank shakes his head. "I best wait with the wagon. See what comes 'long down the road." He stands, puts his hand on the mantel for balance.

"Ain't much in the shape for trekking through that cotton, old man."

The boy returns with the bucket, which he sets down in its place in the corner of the room. Frank looks at him in the shadows, and he knows it's just the shadows but still it's Willie's young face he sees staring back at him. Willie. Frank rubs his eyes. "I best be gone," he says. He nods at the man, at the woman beyond. "Obliged to you."

The woman interrupts her song. "Ain't something I can live with you keel over in the cotton," she says. "You stay the night here." The baby, who had quieted, begins to whimper again at the sound of its mother's raised voice.

"Ma'am," Frank says. "Obliged to you. But my boy's gonna be buried in the morning, and I got to get to St. Martinville tonight."

Gabe

D inner is waiting when they get home: fried fish, potatoes, bright and bitter collard greens. Gabe sits at his usual spot at the kitchen table, his mother to his left, his father to his right. His grandmother sits across from him, though her setting is empty, and she is asleep. Gabe finds it difficult to look at her, the spittle that has collected in the lines around her mouth, the fuzz of her chin, the way her lips fold in over the place where she once had teeth. He stares at his food, which sits mostly uneaten on his plate. He lost his lunch sandwich in a bet with Chub Larson over who could spit the farthest, and he knows he should be hungry, but he can't bring himself to eat. He pushes the fish around with his fork, the crisp brown skin and the flesh, Buddy Cunningham's voice sounding in his ear: *nigger fry, nigger fry, nigger fry.* And he can't help wondering what it looks like, a man being fried to death, whether Willie Jones's skin will bubble and crisp like the batter around a fillet.

He sets his fork down and looks up. His parents both stare at their plates as they eat, their knives and forks clacking. As an assistant prosecutor, his father used to tell them stories at dinnertime, about the thieves and arsonists he tried, about schemes of small-scale embezzlement and insurance fraud, mostly petty crimes. When Polly became DA, Willie's case was his first, and he does not talk about it; the silence is so ringing that Gabe thinks Willie might as well be sitting at the table. Gabe knows his parents have tried to shield him from almost everything to do with Willie Jones, but talk around town has been enough to poke chinks in the armor they've tried to fashion. The details of Willie's case and trial are all still hazy, but they've been slowly coming into distressing focus.

He looks at his father—the lines bleeding back from the corner of his eyes, the hard bone of his nose, the flat space between his eyes, the quiver of muscle along his jaw as he chews—and for a frightening moment Gabe can't find in all those features the father he knows. He can't see the man in the backyard, shirtsleeves rolled up, pitching him a ball, or the man with the fishing rod and tan hat at the edge of the bayou, or the man sitting on the edge of Gabe's bed at night, reading glasses on the tip of his nose. For a frightening moment, studied hard, his father's features combine into the face of someone he can't recognize, someone willing to send a man to death, and he feels himself reel the way he did when he took a slug from the Kane twins' father's flask, the world suddenly shot into the distance. Gabe finds he has to close his eyes.

"Son," he hears, in a moment. His father's voice.

Gabe opens his eyes, and dares to look. His father is his father again.

"Everything OK?"

Gabe nods. He looks down at his food, pushes his plate away.

Lane

Lane doesn't have much of an appetite, but Seward finishes his steak for him, gristle and all. As he watches the captain eat, Lane thinks about the man in the jail cell across town, and wonders if they'd afforded him his choice of a final meal. Lane would choose oxtail soup and collard greens cooked in drippings of fatback if he had to, though he can't imagine having much of an appetite then, either.

His father's last meal was chitterlings and grits. Lane knows this because he was the one who found the man, face-down on the kitchen floor, the plate of food his wife had left out for him half eaten on the counter. At first Lane thought he was sleeping, deep in a drunken coma, but when he went to turn his father over he knew even before he saw the lifeless face roll into the early sunlight that the man was gone; his body had already stiffened coldly into death. The doctor later told them that his heart had simply stopped. His mother said his heart had stopped many years before.

When the captain has finished eating, he pushes abruptly away from the table and tosses onto his empty plate the napkin he'd tucked into his collar. Lane watches as the remaining juices seep into the linen. "Couldn't eat another thing," Seward says. "You?"

Lane shakes his head.

The captain reaches into his pocket for his billfold. "I'll go settle up," he says, standing. "Meet you at the truck."

Lane rises and makes for the washroom at the back of the place. The tavern has grown even more crowded in the course of an hour; the din of music and laughter comes together as a single sound, and the crowd seems a single entity. He keeps his head low and shoulders through, the disorderly mass of bodies a foreign thing around him after months of row by row, and he is sweating when he reaches the washroom. He bends down over the sink, splashes water across his face. It is tinged brown, and smells of the bayou's sulfur depths, but it is cold. He stands, dries his face with his shirt, and then he's face-to-face with his own reflection in the mirror.

He studies it with a deadened interest; it is the first good look at himself he's had since being in prison. Six years he's done hard labor in the prison fields, farming okra, soybeans, wheat, and it has changed him. His shoulders and chest have hardened, and the forearms are ridged and tan. His face is a darker, toughened version of itself; his mouth is a line; his eyes are sunk and hooded. Once he'd woken at the edge of a wheat field, his head bloodied by a forgotten blow, half his ear gone. The other half stands small and jagged against his head; he touches the now familiar countours of the interrupted flesh, seeing it clearly for the first time.

Willie

He keeps his eyes closed as he eats. He sees his mother over a spattering pan in the apron she wears with the wide blue flowers, the one his father gave her for her birthday that year when it got so cold they woke up one morning to frozen dew, the grass outside the door a sparkling silver sea. He sees his mother carrying a tray of fried fish to the table, sees his father at the table's head, the sun setting through the window behind him, the dog sniffing out in the yard.

He sees the old picnic blanket, flies buzzing around potato salad, Darryl and Sadie on the bayou's edge. He sees a rope swing swaying, dark heads in the water, ripples glinting in the sunlight. He sees the tendrils of a willow, fat branches reaching out over the water. He can feel the heat of the sun on his skin.

He sees a pecan grove, the stiff narrow leaves around the bulging husks, the split husks with their treasure on the ground. He sees a giant silver bowl, Grace's thin hand around a wooden spoon, swirling sugar, butter, nuts into a single substance.

He sees as a boy, eye-level with the table, the fire roaring in the hearth, the dog curled at his father's booted feet, his mother's feet bare beneath the hem of a bright green skirt.

He sees his life with every bite. He swallows his memories whole.

Father Hannigan

H annigan stands by the bullpen's window as Willie Jones eats his final meal, a napkin tucked into the collar of his brown shirt. He'd been sitting across from Willie, but the way the boy began to eat—his eyes closed, his face transported— made Hannigan feel as if he were intruding on something personal and profound, on something that needed privacy, so he removed himself from the table.

Sheriff Grazer has left Willie and the priest in the bullpen and gone downstairs. There was a time when Hannigan might have been afraid at the thought of being alone in a room with a convict, but after eight months of spending time with the boy, he has come to think of Willie as a friend. Willie is a danger to no one; it seems everyone agrees—Hannigan, of course, but also the sheriff and the deputies, who allow him to exist daily without shackles, to write notes to his mother with a sharpened pencil, and now to eat a proper final meal, using fork, knife, and all.

Hannigan stands at the window unhappily, looking out over the grass in front of the courthouse and the concrete staircase that leads up to the building's doors, all of it cast in the orange glow of the streetlight out front. There are sixteen steps; for no good reason Hannigan always counts them whenever he goes up or down, as he has done numberless times in the months he's been visiting Willie Jones. A statue of Lady Justice rises from the center of the staircase; it was in the shadow of this statue that Nell approached him yesterday, asking him to bring her in with him.

Hannigan turns from the window and sees that Willie has eaten nearly everything Nell packed in the basket. Sheets of tinfoil are strewn across the table, and the china dishes that held the potatoes and the beans are empty. Only pecan pie remains; Willie has eaten one large slice. He takes the napkin from his collar and wipes his mouth, his eyes now open. Then he puts his napkin on the table and sits back. "Have some pie?" he asks, looking at Hannigan earnestly.

Hannigan hesitates. He looks at the pie, wonders if later, when he leaves with all the dishes, he should wrap it up and save it, or throw it away. Neither seems the right choice. "I'll have a slice," he says. He pulls out a chair as Willie fixes him a piece of pie. Willie cleans his fork with a napkin, sticks it into the pie, and slides the plate across the table. "Thank you, Willie," Hannigan says, and he takes a bite.

Willie rubs his bald head and gives the priest a crooked grin. "Can't get used to it," he says.

Hannigan swallows the sweet mouthful and tries to smile back. "Bet it's cooler, anyway." He prepares another bite of pie, but leaves the laden fork on his plate. Distractedly, he starts to smooth and fold the sheets of greasy tinfoil, picturing Nell's hands on the foil before his, wrapping the dinner up, and he wonders not for the first time why she cares. He'd planned to ask, earlier, but it was all he could do to leave with composure after she asked how he feels about Willie, about tonight.

95

When he looks up, Willie's eyes are on him, watching. "How are you feeling, Willie?" Hannigan asks. A stupid question, really, but what else to say?

Willie frowns. "I don't know," he says. "It don't seem real. Almost *can't* feel."

Hannigan nods. He smooths a sheet of tinfoil, wishing he had brought a deck of cards. "I think I understand that." He folds the foil in half, then into quarters, and then he puts it aside and reaches for another piece to fold, even as he realizes that there is no point, that all this foil will just be thrown away. Still, he smooths and folds, smooths and folds, wondering what you say to people not while they are dying—this he has done, this he can do—but when they are scheduled imminently to die. He has never before ministered to someone on death row.

"Mostly I just want it to be over with," Willie says. "I don't want it to happen, but if it has to happen I just want it to be done. It's like when I did school, I didn't want to take any test, but I wanted test time to hurry up and come so it would be over and I wouldn't have to think about it anymore."

"I understand that, too. And it will be over soon," Hannigan says.

"You're funny, for a priest."

Hannigan looks up. Willie is looking at him quizzically.

"When my mama come she makes us pray. With you we usually just play marjolet."

"I'm not here to convince you of anything, Willie."

"Why not? Ain't that what a priest is supposed to do?"

"Maybe some priests," Hannigan says. "But I'm here as a friend."

Willie seems to consider this. "My mama says when I get up from that chair I'm gonna start a new life with the Lord," he says. "What do you say?"

Hannigan doesn't answer right away. Then, "What do *you* say, Willie?" he asks.

"That I ain't gonna get up from that chair." Willie says this adamantly. He looks into Hannigan's eyes. "Maybe I'm wrong, but I can't see getting up to a whole new holy life. I've tried and tried to make myself believe in all that stuff, but to me it's like believing in Br'er Rabbit."

Hannigan takes a breath, tries to formulate his thoughts, to put together a theory that will be both comforting and one he believes—but he can't do it. "Look," he says. "I'm going to be completely honest with you. I don't know what happens when we die."

"We die. Ashes to ashes."

"Yes, ashes to ashes. For our bodies. But I believe that something must come of our souls. They can't just disappear."

There are sounds from outside: a man shouting, a barking dog. Willie looks toward the window; Hannigan watches him, wonders what is going through his mind. The outside sounds fade, and Willie turns back to the room. "So where do the souls go?" he asks.

"I don't know," Hannigan admits.

"So you say there ain't heaven."

"I didn't say that. I said I don't know."

"You believe in God?"

Hannigan swallows. Slowly, he pulls the china dishes toward him across the table. They are white china, with a blue design of sparrows among leaves, intricate and fine. He

97

scrapes the remaining bits of potato in with the remaining beans, puts the bowl with the scraps into the empty one, slides the bowls aside. He looks at his neglected slice of pie. Then he looks at Willie. "I don't know what I believe," he says, finally. "I think I believe in God, but I'm always looking for a sign." Hannigan has barely admitted as much to himself; he wonders if he's saying this because he knows that the words will die when Willie does. "I believe in goodness, and I guess that's a sign. But I also see the evil that exists in the world. I see the cruel way men can treat each other." He frowns, looking at the boy before him, thinking how in the face of the accusation against him, he never stood a chance. What happened, happened, Willie himself admits this. The question is the name by which it's called: the girl's father calls it rape, and on the stand, Willie called it love. Grace is the only one who can truly answer, and she is not alive to say. "I see what's happening to you," he says, softly.

Willie shakes his head. "No," he says. "I deserve to die. I want to die. It's 'cause of me that Grace is gone."

PART TWO

Lane

Back at the truck, Seward takes the wheel. He drives them to the outskirts of town, over the railroad tracks and away from the water. He's lit the cigar that's hung from his lips for most of the day, and the smoke, oaky and cloying, billows in the truck's cab before whisking out the window. He slows at each intersection to read street names, muttering beneath his breath. "West Pershing," he finally says, satisfied, and turns onto the sought-out street.

The truck bumps along the rutted pavement. Beer cans and broken glass line the curb, where shotgun shacks stand squat, windows open, doors ajar. Local prostitutes have gathered on the porches; through the truck's open window Lane can hear them calling and laughing.

Seward slows the truck down in front of the only commercial building on the street, a single-story, wood-sided building flanked by these shotgun shacks. PIKE'S PLACE is painted in bold black letters shadowed in white along the top of the building, and the windows have been frosted, so that you can't see through the glass. A single lamp affixed to the wood above the black-painted door lights the threshhold; Lane watches the door open and a man stagger from within. He doesn't ask what they're doing here; he's heard about Pike's Place from other inmates who had perked up when they heard that Lane would be accompanying the captain to New Iberia. But he hadn't thought they'd come.

Seward grunts. "Funny, just six years what you can forget. Could used to find Pike's like the nose on my face." He puts the truck in gear and continues driving down the street until they come to a lot where a handful of other cars have parked, by the edge of a cemetery. He pulls in and cuts the engine. For a moment, neither man moves or speaks. Outside, the marble crypts glow in the moonlight. Many of the headstones are old, cracked, and covered with moss, their lettering losing definition, but a few clustered together in one corner are recent and uniform, small white stones beside limp American flags. Seward breathes loudly and pats the side of the truck, draws long on his cigar.

"You can forget a lot," Lane says, finally.

The captain looks at him questioningly.

"Six years."

Seward grunts.

"What happened to her?"

"Happened to who?"

"Your grandbaby." It had stuck with Lane earlier, that detail.

The captain winces. He looks away. "Born and died in a day," he says, pinching the cigar from between his lips. "Took her mama with her. 1937. Year I came to Angola."

"What'd you do before?"

Seward gives a bitter laugh. "Farmer, out in Avoyelles Parish. Didn't have a pot to piss in."

"So you came to Angola."

"That's right. Where the money's at. Used to bring sorghum to load up here at the 'Beria port, made in three years not half what I done made in six."

Lane gestures toward the back of the truck. "And how many men you killed in six years?"

There's a pause. "Killed's a way of puttin' it. Brought justice to's another."

"How many?" Lane asks again.

The captain takes another long drag on his cigar, squinting at Lane down the stubby length of it. "Enough." He tosses the smoldering nub out the window and into the dirt. "Get out," he instructs. Seward gets out of the truck himself and goes around to the back. By the time Lane has joined him the captain has swung the heavy doors of the trailer wide open. He stands there, surveying what's inside in the same posture you'd assume before a work of art, arms crossed, head tilted slightly to the side. Lane glances uneasily around them, but they are alone.

Lane stands beside the captain and looks into the trailer. Back at Angola, he'd seen the chair only from a distance, as deputies loaded it up from the garage on the hill. He'd been struck by how regular it was: for all intents and purposes, a chair. Now close, in the moonlight, he can see all the awful details. The wood along the lower beam is singed in the spots to which ankles have been strapped. The wood is darkened at the end of each arm, stained by the grip of hands sweaty with fear. A crown of metal is bolted to the top, and a black hood is draped over the seat back, to cover a face that shouldn't be seen. Overall, the chair is larger than Lane had judged it to be from afar, made of heavy oak and proportioned so that even a man of Seward's size would be dwarfed. Lane has heard of a boy who'd had to sit on a pile of books while he died so that his arms could rest more easily on the oaken ones. He doesn't know if this is fact or prison lore.

"Get in," the captain instructs.

"Sir?"

"Climb up and get in. Take a seat."

Lane grabs the side of the trailer and hoists himself inside. He looks at the chair's wooden seat, the nicks and scratches and stains, all of unknown, storied origin.

"Sit."

Lane turns around. He sits. The wood of the seat is as hard as the wood of any wooden seat, and the rungs of the ladder-back knock every few knobs of his spine. He thinks of the bodies that have slumped here, scorched and smoking.

"How does that feel?" The captain stands framed in the trailer's doorway, his head glistening in the moonlight. Spanish moss dangles in the view, hanging from a branch Lane can't see.

"Like a chair," he says, finally.

Ora

Ora cleans the dishes with rhythmic ferocity. She feels angry, though she can't quite pinpoint the source of her displeasure. It's Dale, but nothing in particular about him. She doesn't like it when he's bigoted, but it isn't that. She doesn't like it when he chews with his mouth open, but it isn't that. She doesn't like it when he drags his fork against the bottom of the plate, or cleans his teeth after a meal with his tongue, or when he leaves inventory to the last minute, but it is none of these things, either. It is his very self that irks her, which fact irks her further, because he is the man that she is supposed to love. Did love. *Does* love, she tells herself. *Does* love, she insists.

She puts the last dish aside and crosses the kitchen to the door of the store. She pushes it slightly open and peers through the crack. Dale is crouched before the sundries shelf, a clipboard on his knee and a cigarette between the fingers of one hand. His back is toward her, and something about the smooth skin behind his ear, that ageless arc of pink, translucent cartilage, melts her anger into exhaustion.

Quietly, Ora closes the door. She looks across the kitchen toward the hallway and their bedroom, which used to be the living room—and Tobe's bedroom, which was theirs until Tobe was born. Both doors are closed. On their door hangs a cross, and on Tobe's hangs a Yankees baseball cap, as if at any moment he might emerge from within, put it on his head, and go out to wait for the bus that would take him off to school. She tries to imagine that he is in there, listening to music or reading a book, but she knows all too well that he is not.

As has become habit, she enters their son's bedroom. Everything is as Tobe left it seven months ago. A pair of pants still hangs over the back of the room's single chair, and a Louis Armstrong record still rests on the turntable. Everything in here is as Tobe left it seven months ago. There's a pair of shoes on the floor by the nightstand, and an empty water glass beneath the lamp. King Kong beats his chest on a poster above the bed. On the opposite wall is a poster of Winston Churchill, with the words "Let Us Go Forward Together." Ora has grown to hate it.

She turns on the fan and sits on the bed in the semi-darkness, the only source of illumination the dim light from the hallway. She puts her head into her hands, listening to the fan's hum as she stares at her bare feet against the blue-and-white crochet of the rug. There is a stain by her big toe: coffee, from a breakfast in bed years and years ago when the bedroom was still theirs. At the memory, her heart gives an unexpected lurch. Her boys, she thinks, her boys. She lies down and curls onto her side, her head on Tobe's pillow. She breathes in deeply, as she always does, and notices, with a pang, that his smell is fading.

Dale

Peanut butter, instant mashed potatoes, EZ Serve Liver Loaf, jars of tamales. Dale scans the shelves glumly. Not much has sold lately, with the exception of breakfast cereal and mayonnaise. It's hard to know what people are going to buy from month to month; he is never sure just what to stock. This month's mayonnaise might be next month's root beer. Last month it was canned baked beans that everyone seemed to want. He makes a note to get more Waffelos and Cocoa Hoots, wondering if it's the cereal people are after or the giveaways inside, the little stickers, toys, and comics that have started to come with the sugary stuff. No one's picked up any Shredded Wheat.

Dale shifts his weight from the ball of one foot to the other and drags on his cigarette. His knees hurt from crouching, and his nostrils burn with the lingering scent of the Lysol he used earlier to mop the floor tiles, which suddenly beneath the soggy strands of yarn became again the hopscotch squares they were for Tobe ten years ago. That's been happening with a lot of things, since the letter arrived—the squeegee not a squeegee but the tool that Tobe as a boy liked best, the oil drum outside is instead the horse Tobe used to ride.

Dale looks toward the door as a beam of headlights sweeps briefly through the store; a vehicle has pulled into the station. The army men, he thinks. Finally they have come with the news.

The driver parks beside the pump, and when the headlights go off Dale sees that it isn't a military or an official-looking vehicle at all, but a boxy Bantam light truck similar to their own, with headlights perched on the wheel hubs and a small cargo bed covered by a canvas tarp. Little differences make Dale think it's maybe a newer model than theirs: the hood is more compact; the rear wheel fenders are dressed up in chrome. Benny jogs across the lot from his own truck and leans down to the open window, and when he has gone around to the pump on the truck's other side, the driver's door opens and a man climbs out.

At the sight of the man, the dog begins to bark from the shadows by the store. Dale had forgotten about the dog. His bark is muted through the glass of the store door, but it's a deep, chesty sound that Dale finds satisfying. He's never cared for yappers. The driver starts to walk toward the store and the dog runs out from the shadows, into the ring of light cast by the flickering lamp above the pumps, barking and circling. Dale stands up, the clipboard still in his hand, and goes outside.

The heat is staggering. It has the same effect upon Dale, stepping into it, as he remembers bitter cold had when once he visited Chicago in wintertime; it momentarily takes his breath away. He tosses his cigarette onto the dirt and walks toward the pump, waving the clipboard at the dog and shouting reprimands as if it were customary, as if the dog were his. "Hey!" he yells. "Settle down, now. Settle! Hey!"

"It's all right," the man calls out. He squats down and holds out his hand for the dog to sniff. "He's all right," the man says again, as Dale approaches.

"Ain't all right," Dale says. "Can't have him scaring off customers, now."

"Don't have enough gas for a lion to scare us off." The man stands. He's wearing slacks, a white dress shirt, thin black suspenders, and a loosened tie. He holds a snap-brim hat, which he places on his head. "Store closed for the night?"

"Never quite closed," Dale says. He regards the man, then shifts his gaze toward the highway at an approaching car, the muffler busted from the sound of it. The car slows as it passes, as if it might stop, but it doesn't. Dale watches the single working taillight fade down the highway along with his own bitter hope. He half laughs to himself; who would hope what he is hoping for?

Dale turns only when the red pinprick of taillight has disappeared into the darkness. "Come on in," he says. He leads the man toward the store and ushers him inside, goes behind the counter, and sets his clipboard down. Out the window, he sees that the dog is still standing where they left him in the middle of the lot, rigid and alert, eyes trained in the direction of the store as if he were watching the man through the glass. Dale himself looks over at the man, who stands before the cooler, considering his options. He chooses a Double Cola and brings it to the register, setting the bottle on the counter as he reaches into his pocket for coins. "How much do I owe you?" he asks.

"Dime."

The man puts two nickels on the counter. "And the gas?"

"Pay for the gas ouside," Dale says. He slides the coins across the laminate and scoops them into his other hand.

"Year's that Bantam?" he asks, gesturing toward the window with his head as he drops the coins into the till.

"Forty-one, I believe."

"Got a thirty-seven been running rough. Can't rightly figure out why. It's not the camshaft." He frowns. "Spark plugs, maybe, even if they look OK." He sniffs. "Yours run good?"

"Far as I know." The soda hisses as the man removes the cap. His eyes travel to the window. "Truck belongs to the boss."

Dale follows his gaze. He hadn't realized that there was a passenger, but now he sees a second man, dressed much like this one, but older, balding, and stout. He's gotten out of the pickup and is looking into the cargo bed.

"Portable transmitter back there," the man explains. "That's mostly what the truck's used for."

"Portable transmitter?"

"For remote broadcasts—football games, fires, stump speeches, and other such events."

"So y'all are radiomen."

"KVOL, out of Lafayette. We're headed to St. Martinville. Covering the execution."

Dale wonders how you cover an execution on the radio. Seems to him there'll be as little to hear as there will be for old Art to see.

"Well," the man says. "Obliged to you." He nods at Dale and crosses to the door, where he pauses. "We'll be on KVOL and KVCC," he says. "Tune in."

The entry bell clatters as the door closes, and as Dale watches the man cross the lot to the truck, he thinks, of tuning in, that he probably won't.

Polly

After dinner, Polly retreats to his old office with the paper, as he often does. He tips his chair back and puts his feet up on his desk. The news is grim: a time bomb exploded at the post office in Naples, killing over one hundred people; the USS *S-44* was shelled and sunk by the Japanese off Uomi Saki; ninety-seven American civilians on Wake Island were executed by the Japanese and buried in a mass grave.

He doesn't read much beyond the headlines; a few articles he skims. Lately it's been hard to concentrate on anything; he's felt as if his mind were split into two reels, one attending to the business of life, and the other in vague and constant thought about Willie Jones. He starts to skim an article on the record losing streak of the Philadelphia Athletics, but a paragraph in he gives up, puts the paper down. He can't do it. Not tonight.

Polly's office is diagonally across the patio from the kitchen and directly underneath Gabe's bedroom, so most nights after dinner he can both see Nell in the kitchen and hear Gabe overhead. He has always liked that sense of triangulation, the sense that the three of them, though apart, are still connected. He turns around to look out the window behind him; sure enough, Nell is there, drawing at the kitchen table. She sits on the edge of her seat, bent low over the paper. Though he can't see them from here, he can imagine the row of pencils lined up on the table, the dish of shavings, her silvered fingertips. As Polly watches his wife, he listens to sounds of his son: the occasional creak of floorboards over-head, muffled music. Gabe. Polly can still see the look on the boy's face as they were walking home, the confusion as he considered the outcome of legal justice in the case of Willie Jones. Polly has had to steel himself against criticism by some for Willie's sentence. But Gabe—his disapproval, so innocently logical, is crushing.

Slowly, he turns back to his desk and pulls open the topmost drawer. Inside is a postcard that he's kept with him for nearly thirty years, since his father gave it to him as a sort of souvenir—one he didn't want, but one he has held on to nonetheless. He finds the postcard beneath a box of envelopes and takes it from the drawer. It is worn at the edges, the image on the front grainy and old. In the foreground is a gathered crowd, the white faces luminous in the camera's flash, stark against the black night sky. Some are laughing, some appear to be in mid-speech, some seem bothered, and some look blank. The women in the crowd wear flowered, short-sleeved housedresses; their hair is fastened with barrettes. The men wear ties and slacks, their shirtsleeves rolled up. Many are wearing boater hats or fedoras, and several have cigarettes in hand. Most appear oblivious to the carnage overhead, where two young black men hang in bloodied clothing from the branches of a live oak.

Polly can remember how heavily they seemed to hang there, and how their bodies gently twisted, as if there were a breeze. One of the men wore pants, belt, and shoes. His shirt had been ripped open, and though they aren't apparent in the photograph, Polly remembers the oozing wounds across his chest, the buzzing flies. The other man was barefoot, his shirt tattered, and a sheet was tied around his waist. Polly doesn't know what happened to his shoes, or his pants; by the time he and his father had arrived, the two men had been dead for hours.

They stood at the edge of the crowd, his father's hands on Polly's shoulders. Polly remembers wanting to shut his eyes, but staring nonetheless, fearful of his father's disapproval. He's not sure what horrified him more, the casual nature of the crowd, or the men hanging from the tree. It wasn't for another year that his father saw the postcard in a gas station store, on a rack with other postcards depicting cartoon alligators and Main Street, Lafayette. He stares at the postcard now, remembering, and he wonders which is worse, to be lynched or to be shocked to death in an electric chair. There was a time when he was sure there was difference, but now that he's had a hand in it, he wonders if it really matters in the end what kind of justice it is—mob or legal—when the end result is death.

He puts the postcard down and sits back in his chair. He looks up at the wooden planks above his head, and he clings to the thin thread of the melody overhead as a reminder of the silence there might be if he hadn't done what he had to do.

Nell

S he works carefully, methodically, mark by tiny mark, hundreds of thousands of them, which when she's finished will cohere into what others will see as a single image, this one of a tree at the edge of a field. Anyone else would say that her drawings are realistic representations, but to her they are fundamentally abstract, each one a collection of lines, of lights and darks and shapes and shadow. She keeps her head low to the paper as she draws, looking up only to sharpen or change her pencil, thinking of nothing but her work. It is her favorite time of day for this reason; everything—the heat, the war, her worries, the world—recedes, leaving her entirely to herself.

This was how she intended to spend her life—as an artist. She had just enrolled in the Corcoran School of Art, in Washington, D.C., when she met Polly, who was there as a legal intern, and she dropped out to follow him south when his internship was up. She doesn't dislike the south, but even after thirteen years it still feels foreign to her, and as she goes about her duties as daughter-in-law, mother, wife, she has the distinct sense that there is some other version of herself living the life she meant to have.

She changes pencils—dark to light—as, in the image, tree meets sky, and she has barely begun the fine, faint crosshatch of a cloud when the alarm clock on the table jars her with its sudden shrill chime. She turns the alarm off, surprised as she always is by how quickly the minutes pass when she is working. She rises from her chair. Out the window and across the patio, she can see Polly at his desk, and it strikes her, seeing him from behind, how gray his hair has become. It is strange to find themselves beginning to grow old.

In a moment, Nell turns back into the kitchen. From a drawer beneath the counter she takes a needle, plunger, and glass tube, into which she drops a small, white pill of morphine from a bottle in the cabinet. Deftly, she inserts the plunger and draws water into the tube from a sanitized supply in the fridge, then shakes the tube vigorously until the pill dissolves.

Though once these things might have made Nell shudder, she has become expert in giving injections, in bathing Mother's papery skin and dressing her brittle body. She performs these tasks with swift detachment, and it often occurs to her how familiar it is, to handle another body—to thread an arm through a sleeve or to wash behind an ear—it's just as it was with a toddling Gabe.

She carries the tube and needle with her down the darkened hallway. Quietly, she opens the door to Mother's bedroom and steps inside. The room smells of dust, breath, and old books. Mother is asleep, the lump of her body barely perceptible beneath the bedsheets. Nell crosses the room and turns on the bedside light; the old woman stirs, but she does not open her eyes.

Over the past five years, there have been successive strokes, each one incapacitating Mother further, rendering her deaf, crippling her left arm, then the left side of her face. She has been ravaged, whittled near to bone. When Nell thinks of the hours Mother used to spend in the garden, pulling up henbit and mallow by the roots, and when she thinks of the woman's endless thirst for Gilbey's gin and her cackling sense of humor, this seems a particularly awful way to go, blow by blow by blow. Nell quietly hopes that the next stroke will be the last.

She reaches for Mother's arm, pinches the skin between her fingers so that the needle will not hit bone. The needle slides in almost too easily. She slowly depresses the plunger, thoughts of death inevitably leading her mind back to Willie Jones. If the boy has to die, she thinks, at least it will be quick. But the thought provides less comfort than unease; and the anger that, while she was drawing, had settled to a simmer begins again to boil.

Gabe

The radio is a cathedral shaped Crosley Dual Ten hewn of birch or alder, with four wooden knobs and brass molding around the dial face, a Christmas gift last year. Every night after dinner, Gabe goes upstairs to his bedroom to listen for a while before he goes to bed. Usually he opts for drama programs over music, but tonight's broadcast of *The Green Hornet* is a rerun, so he's tuned it to a Cajun station out of Lafayette. He lies back on his bed and stares up at the ceiling, listening to a two-step duet of accordion and fiddle.

The cracks in his ceiling he knows by heart. In his mind they form a map, delineating the borders of territories that make up a world that he knows does not exist, but that he feels somehow should, so familiar has its geography become. One of these territories, directly above the foot of his bed, looks to Gabe like Massachusetts. His mother is from Massachusetts. Gabe has never been there, though he would like to go. Massachusetts makes him think of waves splashing against a rocky shoreline, of trees whose leaves turn impossible colors. Of stone walls and lakes that freeze, and hills and mountains, which fascinate him. Gabe can't imagine actually standing on land that is not flat in all directions. This is one of the things his mother says she misses most about the north—living in a three-dimensional landscape. His father argued once that their landscape here was nothing if not three-dimensional, but his mother shook her head. "It's flat," she'd said. "It's missing a crucial plane." Gabe's not sure what she meant.

He stares up at Massachusetts, fixing on the tip at the end. He wonders what it's like to live on the very edge of the land. He thinks he'd feel exposed and unsettled, as if at any moment he might be swept away. Here they've got a safe cushion of solid ground extending around them for miles and miles. His mother calls it *landlocked*.

The dance of accordion and fiddle slows to silence. Gabe listens in the momentary quiet for household sounds—dishes being put away, footsteps, murmured conversation, but the house too is quiet. Outside, he can hear the distant lament of a siren, and he wonders what the emergency is, and whose, and where. Gabe frowns. The sound makes him ponder what they will do with Willie's body after he has died, whether they will take it away in an ambulance or a hearse. When Jimmy Gibson was missing in the bayou last year and all those fathers were searching through the water for his body, there was an ambulance waiting at the bayou's edge even though everyone knew the boy was dead. Gabe didn't dare ask why.

Ambulance or hearse: in the end it doesn't matter which takes Willie's body away, yet somehow that detail seems important. The detail *is* important. All of it's important. Gabe takes a breath and sits up, suddenly and definitely resolved. If his father won't take him tonight, he'll find another way.

Father Hannigan

He locks the rectory door behind him, opens all the downstairs windows, removes the collar from his neck, and opens the topmost buttons of his shirt. He unloads Nell's picnic basket in the kitchen, washes the dishes carefully, dries them one by one, and returns them to the basket, and on top of them he sets the rest of the pecan pie. Standing at the kitchen counter, he forces himself to eat: crackers with tuna.

He'd planned to be with Willie up until his execution at midnight, but after dinner Willie had said he'd rather be alone. Alone himself now, Hannigan isn't sure how to fill the time. He wanders through the house before finally settling on the living room sofa; only when he is supine does he realize how tired he is; part of him would like never to have to move from here again.

He doesn't shut his eyes, because he doesn't want to fall asleep; instead he stares at the ceiling, which in the room's dimness appears to have infinite depth, as if it were a space that he might float up into. He thinks of this morning, of Della Biggs and the magnitude of her distress. He thinks of Willie's poor mother, whom he has visited in St. Martinville once before. He wonders if these women will ever recover from their grief, or if they will spend the rest of their lives aching with the singular pain of a mother who's survived her child—the pain that his mother couldn't endure.

He thinks of Willie, his earnest attempts to prepare himself for a death he's never protested against, even as he's plainly denied the crime. He pictures Willie the day they first met, Willie's thin arms waving at him through the bars of his cell, calling him over to ask for a Bible. He pictures the look on Willie's face as he considers a hand of cards. He pictures Willie tonight, eating his dinner, the calendar hanging on the bullpen wall behind him: October, a painting of cotton fields. He can see the dish of potatoes, nearly empty, the pastry crust of the pecan pie, Willie's eyes closed, his brow untroubled. He sees Willie put his fork down, and sit back contented in his chair. He sees the ropy loop of a noose encircle the boy's neck, sees the floor suddenly give way beneath his chair, sees him falling, falling, until *snap!* the rope is taut and Hannigan jerks awake.

He sits up, sweating. He puts his feet on the floor and leans forward. Oh, the whiskey beckons. He can taste its smoky peat, can feel the burning liquid rivering through his veins. What he would do now for that numb descent into oblivion! He stands, walks into the kitchen, takes the untouched bottle of Old Crow from the back of the pantry cabinet, and holds it up to the window. Moonlight glints in the dusty amber of the luring spirit inside, the stuff that smoothed his young adulthood into something he can't remember.

He runs his finger around the wax seal. He should pray, he thinks, he should pray; it was prayer, at first, that saved him from the stuff. But when he shuts his eyes to speak to God, he finds he has nothing to say.

He gets a glass from the cabinet, fills it with ice, and brings both glass and bottle with him to the living room, where he sets them on the coffee table. He sits down on the sofa, and for a moment, he just looks at them in the darkness, the glass, the ice, the whiskey.

Willie

He allows himself to doze after dinner, and he falls into that memory of frost, that morning of his mother's birthday, that morning when ice glistened around each blade of grass outside.

It is winter, and Willie is five or six years old. Darryl is maybe seventeen, and Willie can feel his brother's big hands on his shoulders, gently yet firmly rocking him awake. He opens an eye; Darryl's face looks down at him, the world out the window behind him white in early sunlight. Willie squints his eyes against the glare, puts his arms over his eyes.

"I gotta show you something."

Darryl pulls Willie upright. Willie stands; cold air pools around his feet.

"Here." Darryl flings his pants toward him, a shirt. "Get dressed. Quick."

"What is it?"

"Just dress!"

"I'm dressing." Willie's teeth chatter as he steps into one pants leg, then the other. He pulls on his shirt, then looks around the floor for his shoes. "It's cold!"

"It's cold. I know it's cold. 'Fore it warms up I want you to see."

"See what?"

"Just come on!"

Darryl leads him to the kitchen and opens the back door. Outside, Willie sees a world that has been tranformed overnight, silvered and stilled into a glinting glassy dream. Willie has seen nothing like it before; he doesn't know what he is looking at.

"A frost," Darryl says. "Ain't that something?"

"Frost," Willie repeats. He looks at the brittle icy grass in wonder.

"Ain't been this cold in years," Darryl says, stepping outside. "I remember the first time I saw a frost I thought the grass was covered in ash." He looks over his shoulder, toward where Willie stands in the doorway. "Well, come on!" he says.

Willie steps outside; the light of the yard is blinding after the shadows inside, dazzling. The grass crunches beneath his feet, less like glass than straw. It's like standing in a field of diamonds, Willie thinks, and he shivers. But he does not go inside, not yet; he stays where he is, watching his white breath curl away and slowly mingle with the world's cold air, watching himself breathe for the first time.

Polly

Polly is still sitting at his desk, head in hands, when Nell appears in his office, holding a needle and an empty syringe. She sets these on the desk before him, and he looks up. Nell's arms are crossed; her face is hard.

"This doesn't set well with me, Polly," she says. "I've held my tongue when I shouldn't have, but I've got to say it. This isn't right."

Polly runs his hands through his hair. "This isn't a good night to talk about it, Nell," he says, tiredly.

"No, it's not. It's too late. I should have said something long ago."

"She's my mother," Polly says. "It's not an easy decision to make. On top of everything else."

Nell glares at him. "I'm not talking about your mother, Paul. I'm talking about the boy who's going to die tonight."

Of course she is. Of course. Polly averts his eyes; he cannot hold his wife's condemning gaze.

Nell pulls up a chair and sits across the desk from him, perched on the edge of her seat. "Look," she says. "When you ran for DA, I supported you, even though I knew that it meant bigger cases, longer hours. I supported you because I thought you were a good man. I thought you were a *fair* man. I thought you were after justice, not vengeance. But Polly! The death penalty?"

"Nell. Rape is a capital offense."

"It doesn't have to be."

"But it is."

"Maybe it is in some towns. Maybe in Houma. Maybe in Baton Rouge. But not here. Here, it doesn't have to be." She frowns. "But you made it so."

Polly takes a moment before replying. "Nell," he says. "I didn't have a choice."

"That's rubbish," Nell snaps. "You could have sent him to who knows how long in prison. But you chose to send him to his death. He's a *boy*, Polly!"

"He's a criminal," Polly counters. "He raped that girl."

"Even if he did, you answer me this—what white man would ever be put to death for rape?"

Polly sets his teeth. He looks at the ceiling again, the floorboards of Gabe's room. His eyes burn.

"I thought you were better than the rest of them down here." Nell says this quietly. She sits back in the chair, puts her hand over her mouth. "I thought you wanted to make a difference. I thought that's why you ran for DA at all."

Polly touches the corners of his eyes with his cuffs. "May," he begins. He drops his gaze from the ceiling and looks Nell in the eye.

"What about May?"

Polly clears his throat. "Last May. Gabe came by the office after school, like usual. We were going to walk home. I told him to wait for me on the steps while I made a last phone call." He rubs the prickly stubble on his chin. "When I came out a few minutes later, I didn't see him. Went over to the barbershop. They hadn't seen him. Went to Western

Auto across the street. They hadn't seen him. I looked for him in the square, the pharmacy, the bookstore. I looked in the woman's fashion store, for God's sake!"

Nell is sitting forward again. She listens intently, her forehead troubled.

"I was just about to go inside and call the police when a car pulled up." Polly stops, picturing the scene; he has dreamed about it vividly on so many occasions that he's not sure if now he's remembering a dream or the actual event.

"Go on," Nell prompts.

"It was Earl Montgomery's car. There were four of them. Montgomery, Stout Biggs, Leroy Mason, and Pope Crowley."

He can see that Nell's jaw is clenched, and her eyes gleam with anger.

"They didn't hurt him," Polly continues. His voice cracks. "They didn't hurt him," he repeats, "but they took him. And they could have hurt him. They could have done worse. And they told me that if I didn't do what they wanted me to do, what they'd done just now was to show me what they could do and would do."

"Those bastards," Nell says. "Those goddamn redneck ignorant pieces of trash." Her look transforms from anger into incredulity. "But what about the police, Polly? What those men did's illegal! Kidnapping! Coercion! Didn't you ever consider going to the police?"

"Nell. What are the police going to do about it when most of them feel the same way?"

Nell is quiet. "Why didn't you at least tell me?" she asks, finally.

Polly looks out the window. Across the street, the Gild-orfs' windows are bright; they appear to be having a party. "I suppose there were a couple of reasons," he says. "I didn't want you to worry. I felt responsible. Responsible and guilty. I know how you felt about me running for DA—"

"I—" Nell starts.

Polly lifts his hand. "I know you supported me, but I also know it wouldn't have been your preference." He lowers his hand. "And then—the fact that my taking the position, taking on this case, should put Gabe in any kind of danger . . . I was afraid you never would forgive me." He half smiles, rubbing an eye. "So I did what I felt I had to do."

Nell sits back. "And here we are," she says.

"Yes," Polly says, and he sits back too. He sighs, nods slowly. "Here we are."

Frank

The two men walk through the cotton field without speaking. Frank walks down one row, the father—his name is Lester—down the next. The cotton plants rustle around them as they pass; brittle stems snap. They walk in silence until they come to the edge of the first field, where Lester stops, unscrews the cap of a canteen he's brought along. He holds it out to Frank. Frank shakes his head.

"You sure?" Lester asks.

Frank nods.

Lester shrugs and brings the canteen to his mouth.

Frank looks back toward the cabin; they have come less far than he thought. He imagines the family inside, the mother settling the children on their pallets, pacing in the shadows with the infant as she awaits Lester's return. Outside, the laundry wavers on the clothesline like so many blue ghosts.

"How old's your boy?" Frank asks, still staring in the direction of the cabin.

"My boy?" Lester wipes water from around his mouth.

Frank nods.

"Amos just a baby," Lester says. "Manny goin' on ten years old."

"Manny," Frank repeats. "I looked at him back at the cabin, saw my Willie." He gives a half laugh, weary. "S'pose now I'm bound to see him everywhere."

"Ain't right for an ol' man to bury his child," Lester says.

Frank looks at him, but he says nothing, shifts his gaze to the wagon in the distance. He's got a vague memory from boyhood, his father crouched over his baby sister's grave, his broad back shuddering. Though he feels nothing now but the urgency of getting where he needs to be, he knows that this same grief must be inside him somewhere, and he's afraid to feel it. "Lot of things ain't right," he says.

"Yassah, I reckon that's the truth."

Again, Frank says nothing. He sets off through the cotton, following his own shadow through the moonlit rows.

"Ain't my business," Lester says, after several minutes. Frank glances at him sideways, waiting for him to continue, but he doesn't pursue his thought right away.

"Ain't my business," he starts again, a few minutes later. "But what you gonna do once you back at the wagon?"

Frank shrugs. "Maybe now the mule will go."

"What if she don't?"

"I tole you," Frank says. He stops walking. He finds it too hot to walk and talk. "Gonna wait, see what comes on down the road."

Lester scratches his head, and Frank notices his fingers, how long they are, thin as pencils. "Not a whole lot come down that road. Been better y'all were on the highway yonder." Lester gestures behind them. "But not a whole lot come on down that road. Least not at night."

Frank does not reply. He has not thought about what will happen should no one come down the road, just as he did not consider what would happen if there were no mule at the cabin. It's one of the things that make Elma crazy. He doesn't think enough ahead, she says. But it seems foolish to Frank to think too far into a future that can only ever be uncertain. The present moment is what's real, and that's where he puts his attention. "All I can do is all I can do," he says. And he continues on through the moonlight.

Gabe

G abe sets out on foot, and follows the Abbeville Highway west out of town. In leaving town to the north or south, it's a gradual transition from city to countryside; city buildings give way to the larger outskirts homes, which themselves give way to mills, sugar plants, sand pits, and refineries, until finally there's nothing left but a landscape of swamp and field. In going westward out of town, though, the change is abrupt: cross over the Old Spanish Trail and all of a sudden there's nothing but field, road, and moonlight, every now and then a live oak adrip with Spanish moss.

Gabe walks quickly, anxiously. The Abbeville isn't a well-traveled highway, especially at night, yet every time a vehicle does pass, Gabe scrambles down the road's slight embankment and crouches low enough so he can't be seen.

The Cunninghams live a couple of miles outside town and down a dirt road off the Abbeville that runs parallel to the Armenco Branch Canal. Gabe turns with some relief onto this road and slows his pace. To his left is the canal; off to the right a sweeping plain of sugarcane stretches into the night, the grasses still and silent. Gabe's been to the Cunninghams' farm only once, last spring, when all the boys went out to shoot the Beretta 22-gauge Buddy's daddy bought in Baton Rouge, but he's come to the canal plenty of times with a fishing rod. Gnarled wax myrtle and prickly fans of dwarf palmetto grow along the water's edge, which tonight is loud with the music of amphibians: the bullfrog's bass honking, the tree frog's strumming call, the high-pitched percussion of the southern cricket frog. Buddy Cunningham says his daddy can catch the canal's bullfrogs with his bare hands and most nights they eat them fried. Gabe wasn't sure whether to believe this until Buddy brought some of the meat to school in his lunch pail, and if it wasn't frog, it wasn't any other kind of meat Gabe recognized.

He follows the road between canal and field until it ends in the clearing where the Cunningham homestead stands. The house is an old dogtrot, and there are people sitting out on the porch, dark shapes from a distance. Chickens wander freely in the driveway, where a run-down pickup and a rusted jalopy are parked; the birds go wild as Gabe walks toward the house.

The figures on the porch turn at the squabbling commotion, and their features come into focus as Gabe nears. Both of Buddy's parents are out there; and Amos Hicks, who used to run a sundries store in town; and a fourth man Gabe doesn't recognize. They're all in wooden chairs, the fourth man sitting on his backward, all of them fanning themselves with scrapped shingles, watching. Gabe is again possessed of the odd sensation that he's not moving of his own volition so much as being moved.

"What have we here?" Mr. Cunningham says, when Gabe has reached the edge of the porch. He rights his tipped-back chair, but he doesn't stand up. Perspiration glistens on his forehead.

"Whattya doin here, Livingstone?" This voice comes from a doorway off the porch, where Buddy has appeared.

He's wearing the same overalls he was this afternoon, and dirt is still smeared across his forehead from when he earlier slid face-first into home. He was out. "Huh?" he demands.

"Hey, Buddy." Gabe nods at Buddy, then at his parents. "Mr., Mrs. Cunningham." He clears his throat. "Thought if it was OK I'd go with y'all tonight," he says. "Over to St. Martinville see that nigger fry." He feels his face grow hot, saying this last.

Mr. Cunningham snorts. "Oh you did, did you," he says. He lifts an eyebrow and looks over at Buddy. "You been running your mouth, boy?"

Buddy grimaces and holds his arms over his chest. "Kiss off, Livingstone!" he shoots at Gabe. Then, "Ain't been talking," he says to his father. His tone is petulant.

"You said your daddy was gonna go over see that nigger fry!" Gabe exclaims, feeling his face grow ever hotter. "Said you were going, too."

"Oh, I'm a go see that nigger fry all right," Mr. Cunningham says. "Ain't gonna miss that more'n I'm gonna miss my whiskey come evening. But ol' Buddy, here—" He looks at the boy in the doorway. "Dint know ol' Buddy here was planning to come along."

"Well, I am," Buddy says.

Father and son hold each other's gaze, their faces hard. But then Mr. Cunningham's face softens. He nods. "All right," he says, and an eyebrow lifts again.

Buddy opens his mouth in surprise.

Mr. Cunningham mimics his son's expression. "I said all right," he says. "You want to go, we go."

"'Bout Livingstone?" Buddy asks, suspiciously.

Mr. Cunningham regards Gabe quietly. "Well, now, why does Livingstone want to go?" he asks.

Gabe hesitates. "My pa won't take me," he finally answers.

"There room in the truck?" This is the man Gabe doesn't know; his voice is low and gravelly.

"Boys really want to come, we kin take the car. Ain't that right, Amos?"

"Reckon that's all right," Amos Hicks says.

Through all of this Mrs. Cunningham has sat stony and expressionless; now, she stands and wordlessly walks inside. The men watch her go. At the thought of his own mother, Gabe is seized by a pang of guilt. But just briefly, because the man with the gravelly voice begins to speak.

"Livingstone," he drawls. He's a large man, his long body fairly draped over the back of his chair. It looks, beneath him, like the chair of a child. He looks at Gabe appraisingly. "You the DA's boy?"

The question makes Gabe uneasy.

"Hmm?" the man prompts.

"Yes sir."

"Bold man," the man says. "Fine lawyer." Gabe feels a surge of pride that is quickly tempered by the sickening effect of the man's next words. "Got that nigger just what he deserves."

The image of his father at the dinner table—the transformed version—flashes before him now, and though he tries, Gabe finds he cannot picture the father that he knows, or the one he thought he knew.

Mr. Cunningham speaks next. "Heard he took a little convincin', myself," he says, to the tall man. "Though I s'pose that don't change the outcome."

"Best hush on that, Walt," Amos mutters.

"What y'all talking about," Buddy demands, from the doorway.

Mr. Cunningham pushes back his chair and stands. "Lawyer talk," he says. "Ain't important." He looks at his watch. "I reckon we best go. Pope's waitin' on us for a ride over, and he ain't the real patient type."

Lane

The inside of Pike's is dimly lit, hazy with the smoke of cigarettes. The room is twice as long as it wide, with low ceilings that make the space feel smaller than it actually is. Dark booths line the length of one wall, and an oak-paneled bar runs the length of the other. Behind it, liquor bottles rise in tiers against a mirror so tarnished it offers only a dim reflection. The absence of music strikes Lane, though the murmur of conversations is a music of its own.

Seward leads Lane toward two empty bar stools, hoists himself onto the cracked red Naugahyde of a seat cover. "Have a seat," he says, patting the bar stool beside him. Lane obeys. The captain lifts a finger at the bartender, who is dunking, rinsing, then setting out glass after glass to dry on a rack behind the bar. He is a large, one-armed man with a thick gray beard; the shirtsleeve of his missing arm has been removed and the shoulder opening sewn tight. He glances toward Seward and Lane, but he seems disinclined to attend to them until he has finished what he is doing.

When the bartender has put the last glass onto the rack, he walks over, puts a large hand flat on the bar. He drums each finger once and clears his throat, looking from Seward to Lane and back to Seward again. His eyes are dark beneath the coarse white tufts of his eyebrows. "Kin I getch you?"

"Whiskey, double," Seward says.

The bartender's eyes glide from the captain to Lane. "You?"

Lane shakes his head.

"Kid's teetotaling tonight." Seward chuckles.

The bartender blinks, expressionless. He pours Seward's whiskey and pushes the glass across the bar.

Seward sips his whiskey, grimaces. "Who do we see about some ladies?" he asks.

The bartender puts a cigarette between his lips, lights it with a match struck against something beneath the bar. "Booth in the corner," he answers. He regards Seward with something like distaste, then disappears to the other end of the bar, where two men are waiting for drinks.

The captain turns to Lane. "Wait here," he says.

Lane watches Seward limp across the room toward the booth, where a man sits bent over a magazine. As Seward nears, the man stands up, and after a moment of conversation, the two shake hands. Lane can't hear them from across the room, but he feels despite and deep within himself a hot thrumming of anticipation. He looks up at the clock hanging at the back of the bar; it is nine o'clock. He thinks how twenty-four hours ago he was lying on a stiff cot in the sweltering heat. Someone in a nearby cell was singing a song he didn't know. Then he fell asleep and had a dream about his mother that he can't remember. And now it is nine o'clock again, and at twelve a man will die, and here they are. Here they are.

He looks back toward Seward and the man, who now stand above a booth where three women sit, their faces flashing in candlelight. Based on what he'd heard about Pike's back at Angola, Lane would have expected black sequins, pasties, lace, the type of outfit you'd see at a brothel in New Orleans. But the clothing these women wear is unremarkable—tie-waist dresses, nylons, low heels. They look, for the most part, ordinary, their hair fashioned in similar bobs, their features plain.

Then, one of them stands. She begins to walk across the room toward Lane, her wide hips moving like a pendulum, her breasts trembling above the V of her neckline. Lane feels his mouth go dry, and drops his eyes.

He looks up only when he has to, his chin lifted by a cold finger, and then he is looking into the woman's black eyes. "Hey, baby," she says, and her smile reveals crooked rows of teeth. She tilts her head and pushes herself between Lane's legs; she smells like vanilla and whiskey. "Come on, baby," she says. "Fat man says to come along with me." Lane thinks to protest, but before he can speak the woman reaches out to touch his face, then runs a finger down over his chest toward his belt, and he feels his body surge with a hunger that he knows he can't deny.

Willie

On his hard cot, Willie hovers in the space between wakefulness and sleep, his mind drifting from that cold, frosty morning when he was young to the afternoon he shared the memory with Grace: the tall grass around them, the rough bark of a tree against his back, the heat of the dappled sunlight filtering through leaves, the sound of the bullfrogs in the bayou, the touch of her hand on his neck flooding him with a rush of feeling so powerful it ached.

He opens his eyes, thinking he'd give anything to feel that ache again. But in here, he is numb to everything but waves of grief, guilt, and fear. He blinks. Eighteen bars to his cell. Ten bars across the window. Six water stains on the ceiling. One hundred twenty tiles to the floor. The rate of dripping from the leaky sink varies, but always the faucet drips. It will continue to drip even after midnight, when he is dead.

He lets his eyes blur. Eight months here have felt longer than all the life he'd lived before. He remembers that life, but he can't remember how it felt to live it. He knows that he came home to warm food and a soft bed, but he can't taste his mother's cooking or feel the give of a mattress beneath his weight. He knows that he liked to go barefoot in mud, but he can't feel the slick wet between his toes. He knows that he held Grace in his arms, but he can't feel her warmth and weight, can't summon that overwhelming ache—the irresistible ache of love, which led them to their fates. It's like the memory of pain once pain has subsided. It's a memory. The pain is gone.

Dale

After he has closed up the store for the night, Dale takes a long, cold shower. He tilts his face toward the showerhead, lets the water batter his cheeks, his forehead, feels it bead on the webbing of his lashes. He imagines that he can feel each individual drop, a million needles of cold tattooing his face numb. As he stands there, a memory surfaces: dazzled sunlight, the ceaseless fall of water from a rock face, glassy sheets breaking into shards that shattered further as they fell cold against his body. He'd been maybe seven, eight years old. Where? He can't remember, but he can hear his father's voice through the plash of water, can hear his father singing: *The cleansing spring, I see, I see; I plunge, and oh it cleanses me!*

Dale wipes the water from his eyes, blinks them open. Mildewed tiles, fluorescent light. He turns the faucet off, steps out of the shower, and dries his face with a towel that he then wraps around his waist. He thinks it might have been Tennessee, that waterfall, but it is one of those memories that are similar to dreams: there, yet just beyond reach.

He gathers the day's clothing from where he left it on the floor and tosses it all into the hamper, and he's about to switch the bathroom light off when he remembers the letter in the pocket of his shirt. For a moment he considers leaving it there, for Ora to find and read when she does the laundry, but it isn't a real thought. He finds his shirt in the hamper and retrieves the envelope from the breast pocket. Once crisp, it is now soft and worn, slightly curved according to the contours of his chest. He has read the letter only once since it arrived in the mail, but he finds himself now opening the envelope again, as if in a week's time the words inside might have somehow changed.

> Your son, Tobias, was killed in action on September 18, 1943, on Attu Island.
>
> The Japanese made a counterattack through our right lines. Tobias was on duty as a member of a 37-mm gun crew when the position was rushed by a large group of Japanese.
>
> I know that nothing can make amends for the great loss you have sustained. But I wish to convey to you the deepest sympathy of the officers and men of this organization in your bereavement. Tobias was held in high regard by all members of the command and was a splendid soldier.
>
> His loss is felt deeply by the company.

Dale stares down at the words, thinking of the moment by the mailbox when he'd first read them, entirely unprepared. He'd just put a piece of chocolate into his mouth. Chocolate. He can't remember now if he swallowed it, or spat it out.

He folds the letter up and puts it back into the envelope, but instead of bringing it with him to the bedroom, he opens the medicine cabinet and slips it beneath the paper lining of the shelf where he keeps his things: shaving cream, soap, razor. He doesn't want to carry it around with him anymore, as if the truth could be so easily put down.

Dale turns off the bathroom light and walks down the hallway toward the bedrooms. Tobe's bedroom door is ajar, and when he peers inside he sees Ora, curled on their son's bed. Dale watches her, the gentle rise and fall of her rib cage, the strands of hair wavering with each passing revolution of the fan. He feels his pulse tick with some odd mixture of longing, love, and pain. What he'd like would be to go and lie beside her, take her body in his arms, but he knows she wouldn't have him.

He goes into their own bedroom instead, pulls on a T-shirt and boxer shorts without turning on the light. The room is airless. Before lying down he lifts the shade and opens wide the single window, which had been shut against the day's heat. Suddenly the room is flooded with the ruckus of cicadas screeching in the field beyond. Not with cooler air, though; not with any breeze. Dale puts his palm against the screen; the wires are still hot.

He has just turned from the window when he hears another sound from outside, the growling of a dog, a throaty noise, which soon transforms into a steady and insistent bark. Dale frowns and peers outside. He can see little in the shadows behind the station, but someone's out there, he's sure; the dog's bark is now verging on frantic. Suddenly galvanized, his gloom forgotten, Dale pulls on a pair of pants, grabs the .22 he keeps loaded on the topmost closet shelf, and walks swiftly out the bedroom door.

The kitchen is dark. Dale curses when he stubs his toe on the leg of a chair as he hurries across the room; he hasn't bothered to find shoes. He turns on the kitchen light and shoves open the door to outside with such force that it swings crashing into the building's outer wall as he stumbles onto the dirt. He strides past the dog toward the chicken coop, where the hens are in noisy outrage. Rifle raised, he scans the moon-cast shadows for whatever person might be out there, and then he sees a disturbance in the cotton, a rustling of leaves.

"Hey!" Dale shouts, as a head rises from the rows and starts to run away. He squints down the barrel of the rifle, righteous, overcome by anger that startles even himself. "Take another goddamn step and I'll blow your nigger head off!"

It's a kid; Dale realizes this as two scrawny arms lift in surrender. The kid turns around, eyes wide and white.

"Git back here," Dale commands.

The kid obeys. The chickens are hysterical; their noise makes Dale want to shoot each one.

"So you're the one gone and thieved that hen," he growls, gun aimed at the boy as he steps into the dirt yard. The dog has ceased his barking; he approaches the kid with his tail wagging. "Git!" Dale shouts at the dog, lunging toward him and gesturing briefly away with the tip of the rifle; the dog cowers and skitters off toward the shed. He points the rifle toward the kid again. "That right, boy? You thieved that hen and now you're back for another."

The kid shakes his head. "No, sir, I ain't bothered your hens."

"Oh, no? What, skulking round here by night for what then? Huh?" In a single, quick motion Dale lowers the rifle and takes it by the barrel with one hand, while with the other hand he grabs the kid by the collar, drags him toward the light coming from the kitchen.

"Look at me, boy," Dale says, and he squints harshly into the boy's eyes. His breaths are shallow in his anger, and his heartbeat is loud in his ear. "You gonna have to make even with me, you hear that?"

"Sir, I—"

"Don't think you can sir your way out of this, you thievin' little—"

"Dale." Ora's voice is cold, steely, hateful; she herself is an angry silhouette in the kitchen doorway. "You let that boy alone." She steps down into the dirt, and her features are suddenly illuminated by the light. Her eyes are blazing.

Dale does not release his grip on the boy's collar. "I damn well—"

"Dale. I said you let that boy alone." Ora spits the words. She glares at Dale. Her eyelids seem to twitch.

Dale drops the kid's collar, roughly, and glares at Ora. "They're your damn chickens, anyway," he says. The boy stands there, looking from Dale to Ora, taking small steps backward toward the cotton.

"He's not here for the chickens, Dale."

"Oh no?"

"No, he's not. He's here for candy. He's here for candy, and there you go off with your gun—"

"Candy?"

"—and using your nasty words on a child, Dale, a—"

"*Candy?* You been handing out *candy?*"

Ora puts a hand on her hip. "And why shouldn't a boy have some candy?" she demands. "Why shouldn't we be neighborly with our neighbors?"

"They ain't *neighbors*, Ora," he says, gesturing to the spot where the boy used to be, though he has disappeared. "You go round handing out food like that they just gonna come round." he says. "God damn it, you can't go filling your empty nest with niggers and canines."

The moment the words leave his mouth Dale regrets them. He stands there, waiting, wary, looking guardedly at his wife. But she does not yell. She just stares, her eyes hard, resolute. She takes a long breath, then strides off barefoot into the cotton. Dale doesn't call after her. He doesn't dare, even though he thinks he'd give anything for her to stay.

Ora

Ora isn't sure where she's going, or what she's doing; all she knows is that standing there in the yard with Dale she had to get away, and she damn well wasn't going back inside the station. She walks briskly through the rows of cotton, ignoring the stalks and sticks among the dirt clods that no doubt are bloodying her feet. She doesn't care. She doesn't care, either, about the dry bolls scraping her bare legs, or that the fabric of her skirt will likely tear.

I don't care. I don't care. I don't care. She repeats the words to herself over and over as she pushes blindly through the field, one word for every step until she has come to the far end, where she sinks down in the clearing beneath a single tree. There, she allows herself to weep, not the silent tears she yields to at the station, but in gasping, noisy, childish sobs, because there's no one there to hear her.

When finally she can't cry anymore, Ora rests her head back against the rough bark. She can feel the cuts on her feet now, the scratches on her shins, the throb and sting. But she still doesn't care. She looks across the field to where the station stands in the distance, just a blip on the flat horizon. She imagines going back. She imagines washing off in the tub, having a glass of water, putting on a nightshirt. She imagines slipping into bed, lying through another hot night, and waking to face another hot day—of what? Chickens, hogs, Dale, the store. It used to be enough. When Tobe was home, and even before Tobe, it was a life where she found meaning. But her sense of purpose went with Tobe to war.

She closes her eyes; her body shudders with each breath, the aftershocks of anguish.

After some time, she hears footsteps, but she is ready now. She will allow Dale to offer a hand, pull her up. She will not speak, but she will allow herself to be led home, back to the station. She is too tired to do anything else. She waits calmly for Dale to speak, but it is a boy's voice that she hears instead.

"Ma'am?"

Ora opens her eyes, turns her head. The boy is standing at the edge of the clearing. Though she was expecting Dale, she is not altogether surprised. "Well, you and I sure are seeing a lot of each other today," she remarks. She dries her tears against her shoulders.

"You lost this." The boy holds out the ribbon that had been holding back her hair. "In the field."

"Thank you," she says, and takes the ribbon from him. She gathers her hair behind her and ties it back in place. Then she looks at the boy with disapproval. "I tol' y'all to hold on to that last piece of candy," she scolds. "Y'all were s'posed to save it for tomorrow. Very least wait till morning before coming back for more. Get yourself in all kinds of trouble, this hour."

"I did save it!" the boy says, and he produces the candy from his pocket. "See here?"

Ora looks at the candy in his hand. "Then what did you come back for?"

The boy looks at the ground, scrapes at the dirt with a bare toe. Then he looks up. "You said not to keep away," he offers, unconvincingly.

Ora's eyebrows lift. For a moment, she only regards the boy, unspeaking. "Why'd you really come back?" Ora asks, gently. "This time of night?"

The boy looks at the ground again.

"You can have all the eggs you like," Ora continues. "Not the chickens, but all the eggs you like. Just need to ask, hear? Thievin's not real neighborly, but I'm glad to share."

The boy's head jerks up. "Ain't been thievin', ma'am." His tone is adamant. "On my mama's life."

Ora sighs. "What's yer name, anyway, son?"

"Manny," the boy replies.

"Manny." Ora nods. "I'm Ora. Now, Manny, if you weren't thievin', and you weren't back for more candy, then what were you creeping round for?"

Manny looks at Ora, pulls his mouth to the side. "Don't much matter anymore, now," he says.

"Matters to me," Ora replies. "If we're gonna be friends, matters to me."

Manny bends down to scratch at a scab on his knee. "Just thought y'all might be able to give some help."

Ora frowns. "Help?" She tilts her head, looks at the boy quizzically. "'Course I'll help," she says, "if I can. Here, sit." She pats the ground beside her. "Tell me the trouble."

Frank

Bess stands very still at the side of the road, exactly as Frank left her. The only thing moving is an ear, which moves forward, back, forward, back, as if gathering up the sound of the men's approach.

Lester empties the rest of the water from the canteen into the feed bucket, which Frank has set at the animal's feet. Bess seems to watch as the water spills from the canteen's mouth, a glassy liquid ribbon that shatters against the bottom of the bucket. The men watch it, too, twisting through the moonlight.

Bess lowers her head and drinks, the big lips unfurling. Frank knows well the feel of those lips, their soft, tiny hairs like a whisper against the palm of his hand. The thought of them floods him with a sense of loss; he knows Bess's time is up.

After drinking only a little, Bess lifts her head.

"That it, ol' girl?" Franks asks her. He runs his hand down the side of her neck. He can feel her brittle age. The mule sighs, blinks. Frank nods once. "You know best," he says, conceding. He drags the bucket to the side of the wagon. Water sloshes at the bottom. "Knows her needs," he murmurs. "Knows her limits, knows her needs." He dries his hands on his pants legs.

"Think she'll go?" Lester asks. He looks at Frank doubtfully, the empty canteen in his hand.

Frank shifts his gaze from Lester to the mule. "Think

this here mule done all she was made to do. Ain't gonna ask for any more. Asked too much already."

"Ain't gonna even try?"

"Had this mule twenty years." He shakes his head. "She ain't gonna go."

"So what do you reckon you'll do?

"I'm gonna wait." He glances at the moon, gauging the time. Just a couple of hours until midnight. Soon, if nothing comes along, he'll start walking. He may have promised Elma to get the boy a stone, but he'll be damned if he doesn't see Willie one last time.

One last time. The words echo through his mind, inconceivable.

"Look," Lester says. "Whyn't you come on back to the cabin? You say mule ain't gonna go, mule ain't gonna go. But I say nothin's gonna come 'long down this road. Not at this hour, least. Get some sleep, man. We get your stone where it needs to go come mornin'."

Frank shakes his head. "Go on back to your family. Reckon I'll stay here."

"It don't seem right to leave you."

"I be all right."

Lester looks doubtful. "If you won't come back, least sleep some in the wagon bed."

Frank nods. "I will," he says. "Obliged to you."

They shake hands, and Lester turns and walks into the field. Frank watches him go. Then he sits down on the open tailgate of the wagon and rests a hand on the smooth slab of granite, which, despite the heat, is cool, hard, and cruel beneath his touch.

Ora

The Bantam is in the garage, where Dale's been fiddling with it. It is dank inside, nearly cool in comparison with the outside air, and it smells of whatever solvent Dale uses to degrease, an odor that always makes Ora's head spin. She finds the keys hanging above the worktable and climbs into the driver's seat, but when she tries, the truck won't start. She tries with the choke, without the choke, tries with and without gas, takes the keys out and puts them back in and tries again. Still, it won't start. She hits the steering wheel with her fists in frustration; all she wants is to do this thing the boy has asked, because she can, because it's *something*, a departure from her life. *Damn it*, she mutters. She sits there for a minute, breathing. Then she gets out of the truck and goes back into the heat outside.

She walks around to the station's back door. She passes quietly through the dark kitchen and down the hallway to their bedroom, where she sees Dale asleep in a pair of boxer shorts atop the sheets. She goes to the bed and looks at him; even in sleep, he seems worried, unhappy, and she feels a quick stab of something—love? sadness? tenderness?—pierce her body.

"Dale," she whispers, and touches his shoulder.

He wakes up at once. "Ora," he says. He sits up and puts his feet on the floor. "Ore," he says, "Ore." He pulls her close into him and wraps his arms around her, his head against her thighs. "I'm sorry," he says, squeezing her. "Oh, Ora, I'm so sorry."

Ora lets him hold her, surprised by this. Then he loosens his grip around her legs and looks up at her.

"Dale," she says.

"What is it?" He grabs her hands.

"Truck won't start."

His face transforms: confusion, dismay. "What do you mean, truck won't start?"

"Just like I said." She takes a step backward.

Dale reaches over and turns on the light, frowning. "Look, I'm sorry I said what I did. I'm sorry I did how I did. I love you. I hope you know I love you."

Ora regards him, puzzled. "I'm not leaving you, Dale," she says. "Lord knows I don't know where I'd go."

Then they are quiet, just looking at each other, and Ora can see that Dale is trying but unable to make sense of things. "I just need the truck, is all," she says, finally. "Can't get it to start."

Dale reaches for the T-shirt on the floor. "What do you need the truck for?" he asks, hardening into himself again. He glances at the clock on the nightstand. "It's nearly ten o'clock."

She doesn't answer.

"Ora, you can hardly drive. What do you want with the truck?" He pulls the T-shirt on.

"I can drive just fine," Ora retorts, blushing.

Dale stands.

Ora looks at him, beseeching. "Please just get the truck to start."

153

"You want me to start the truck, you best tell me why."

"Dale," she whispers. "Just do this one thing for me. Please. This one thing is all I ask." Tears gather, and she quickly swipes them away, but not before Dale notices.

He studies her, and he looks both frightened and concerned. Again, he reaches for her hands. "Ora," he says.

She shuts her eyes. "Please," she says. "Dale. Please. Just start the truck."

Dale

The truck won't start because he disconnected the battery when he took the spark plugs out this afternoon. He reconnects the cables now, tightens the terminal clamps with a wrench. He works quickly, watching his hands as if they were things separate from himself, efficient, swift, solid, unaffected by the nebulous sense of dread that has the rest of him shaking, that prompted him to grab the .22 he'd left just inside the door. He lowers and latches the hood and looks at his wife. "Wish you'd tell me what's going on," he says. His voice is reedy. "This have to do with that boy?"

Ora stands in the garage doorway, fierce. She wipes loose hair from her forehead with the back of her wrist. "Tell you when I get back," she says.

"You think you're going anywhere alone, you got another think coming."

"I don't ask a whole lot, Dale."

"No you don't."

"Dale—"

"You're not driving anywhere alone." His tone is harsher than he means it to be. "Not at this hour of the night, you're not." He looks at Ora, can see her jaw grinding, the rising of her shoulders, the familiar angles of her bones. It occurs to him that this is it, that Ora is all that he has left. He inhales deeply through his nose, then gestures with his chin toward the truck. "Get in," he orders, reaching for the rifle and putting it into the truck bed.

Ora's eyes flicker. She crosses the garage and climbs into the passenger side of the truck. The door slams behind her. Dale gets in behind the wheel and gently shuts the door.

"One thing, Dale," Ora says, looking straight ahead, into the shadows of the garage. "If you're coming with me, you're coming with me. You best not get in my way."

Dale turns the keys in the ignition. The engine growls to life.

"You hear me, Dale," Ora says, raising her voice. "You're part of this now."

Dale looks at his wife and gives a single nod. He agrees, though he doesn't know to what. He puts the truck in gear and backs out of the garage, where he pauses. "Where am I going?" he asks.

"State road."

Dale steers the truck across the parking lot until he is window to window with Benny's truck. Benny gives him a puzzled look. He's holding a knife and a piece of wood up in front of him, but he's stopped whittling. Dale can hear voices talking on his radio, a gentle murmur.

"We'll be gone a spell," Dale says through the window.

Benny looks at him. "Everything OK?"

Dale nods. "Be back." He puts the truck in gear and pulls up to the highway; in the rearview, he can see Benny watching them, still just holding the knife and wood. He looks at Ora. "State road whereabouts?"

"Somewhere east of Bileaud. Toward St. Martinville."

Dale turns onto the highway. He and Ora ride in silence. Outside, fields whip by in the moonlight.

"Maybe down here," Ora says, pointing toward a dirt path through a pair of fields, one of several byways that lead from the highway to the state road, which runs parallel.

Dale slows the truck and turns onto the path, which is so rutted that they could nearly walk faster than Dale can drive them. They bounce and lurch; the headlights leap, illuminating field, road, nothing, sky, in flashes Dale finds sickening. "What are we doing, Ore?" he asks. "Please tell me what's going on."

He glances over at her. She's gripping the door handle, her gaze as focused on the road as if she were the one driving. "Man needs our help," she says.

Dale waits for her to explain, but she does not go on.

"OK," he says. "What man? What help? And how do you know?" The truck bounces over a particularly deep rut, and Dale's head slams into the door frame. "Damn it!" He rubs the spot on his head.

He glances again at Ora, who finally turns her head to look at him. "Help we can give," she says, her tone final. She faces forward again. "Got to give help where you can." The state road is just up ahead. "Take a right, here, I'd guess," Ora says.

Dale obeys, and is grateful at least for a level road. "Help we can give," he repeats. He blinks. He is beat, doesn't have the energy to say another thing.

Lane

Lane lies on his back on a bare twin mattress, staring at the ceiling as he regains his breath. His body is limp and glistening. On the floor in the corner of the room there is a single lamp covered by a red cloth, casting an eerie pink light over the room. The blades of the ceiling fan throw dark beams whirling against the pink; his eyes grow heavy watching. His chest rises, falls, rises, falls.

He hears a door open, the flush of a toilet, hears the door close again and feels the mattress sink. "You doin' OK, baby?"

He turns his head. The woman sits on the edge of the bed, touches his chest with her finger. She has put her dress back on. "You OK?" she asks again.

He looks at the ceiling again and nods.

"Now how long it been?" she asks.

"Six years."

She whistles. "Whooo hee, boy. And how much longer you got in there?"

"Got six more."

"Whooo hee. That's rough on a man."

"I don't think about it, much."

"Oh no?"

Lane blinks. "I got other things to think about."

She smooths her dress over her thighs. Voices murmur in the hallway. "Mind me asking what you done?"

"No."

She waits, but he says nothing.

"Then what you done?" she asks.

"Killed a man."

"How come?"

Lane watches the blade shadows sweep, sweep, sweep across the ceiling, wishes that he could feel their air. "I never meant to."

"What do you mean you never meant to?"

"Gun went off and it was done." He turns his head and looks at the woman. She reaches for one of her shoes on the floor beside the mattress.

"Well," she says, as she puts it on. "For murder, twelve years don't seem half bad."

"No," Lane agrees.

The woman reaches for her other shoe.

"What did Seward tell you?" he asks her. "The big man sent you over."

"Seward," she repeats. "He tole me you're a trusty. Tole me you were only out for a day."

"That all?"

"Tole me you were here with the chair to kill that boy." She stands up, looks down at Lane unfazed.

"Don't bother you?"

"Oh it bother me," she says. "It bother me. That boy goin' to his death. It bother me. But I got kids to feed." She looks at the watch around her wrist. "You best get dressed and going, boy. Fat man wanted you back in a half hour's time."

Willie

He isn't sure how long he has been lying there when he hears footsteps coming down the hallway toward his cell. He can tell from the gait that they belong to Sheriff Grazer, and what he feels isn't fear as much as a speeding up, a surge of the heart and a skittering of the mind so quick he doesn't have a chance to register his thoughts.

Grazer appears on the other side of the cell door. "Well, bald Willie," he says, working the key in the lock. He swings the door open and steps inside.

"Is it time?" Willie asks, sitting up. His voice is a near whisper.

The sheriff looks at his watch. "Soon," he says. "But not quite." He tosses a package wrapped in brown paper onto Willie's cot. "Fresh set of clothes," he says.

Willie eyes the package, wondering what it matters, if the clothes he dies in are fresh or dirty.

Grazer opens his hands, as if Willie had spoken his thoughts aloud. "It's the policy, don't ask me why," he says. "Get changed into those and I'll come get you for the ride over." He sniffs, steps out of the cell. He pulls the barred door shut; it hits the door frame with a familiar clank. It's the last time he'll ever hear that noise, Willie thinks, the last time he'll hear the clank and rattle that have kept him these months locked inside. Something about this realization makes his insides plummet the same way they do right before you let go of a rope swing in midair, the terror and excitement indistinguishable.

Grazer pauses before turning to walk down the hallway, gripping the bars of the cell as he looks inside. He shakes his head. "Damn strange to think you gonna be dead in just a few hours' time."

Willie looks at the sheriff in the dim light, thinking of the first time they met, how stunned the sheriff had seemed at the sight of him, as if awaiting a different convict. It seems like a lifetime ago, a lifetime of hunger, heat, boredom, fear. Now here they are. All he has left to suffer is the chair—and then . . . He doesn't know. He can feel his pulse skip at the thought. "I reckon it is," he says, finally, and with shaking hands he reaches for the clothes.

Polly

He finds Nell in the kitchen, bent over her latest drawing. She doesn't seem to notice his presence as he stands behind her, observing her pencil make mark after mark. Before his eyes the marks give shape to a tree, standing at the edge of an already realized field. Part of him wonders if she is mocking him, if soon she will add bodies dangling from the branches, but he knows the tree, knows the field, remembers the picnic they'd taken there last fall to celebrate Gabe's twelfth birthday.

He clears his throat, alerting her to his presence, then crosses the room. He takes the kettle from the stove and fills it at the sink.

"Are you off?"

Polly glances over his shoulder. Nell has put her pencil down and is looking up at him. He shuts the tap off and sets the kettle on the stove. "Soon," he says. He lights the range, and a ring of blue flames whooshes to life. "Coffee?" He turns around.

"No." Nell lowers her eyes and regards her drawing, but she does not pick up a pencil.

Polly sits down across from her. He leans forward, elbows on the table, and rubs his temples.

"Did you say good night to Gabe?"

He looks at the tabletop, ashamed; he hadn't dared. "He was asleep."

"Mmmm."

Polly lifts his eyes; Nell is still staring at her drawing. "Can I ask you something?" he asks.

Nell looks up. "You can ask."

Polly pauses. "Why tonight?" he asks.

"Why what tonight?"

"Why wait until tonight to say anything about how you felt? He was sentenced eight months ago."

Nell drops her eyes. She lifts a pencil from the row of them on the table and moves it from one side of the drawing to the other. Then she moves another, and another, moving the pencils one at a time. "I went to see him yesterday," she says. "Willie Jones."

Polly stares at her.

"I was down there by the courthouse, at the locksmith. I was getting the back door key copied, so I was down there. And then I saw the priest, that Holy Ghost Father, the one who ministers to the black folks at St. Edward's. He was going up the courthouse steps, and I figured there was just one reason he'd be going there, so I asked could I go in with him."

Polly leans back in his chair. "Why?"

Nell shakes her head, faintly shrugs her shoulders. "I had to see him," she says. "I don't know rightly why. But I did." She begins to move the pencils back to the other side of the drawing. "And when I saw him . . ." she trails off, shaking her head.

"He's a criminal, don't forget that."

Nell frowns, lifts a pencil. "That's what I used to tell myself. I told myself he was a rapist, that he had it coming—even if death seemed extreme. But after yesterday . . ." She pauses, taking a deep breath. "I just don't think he's guilty of what they say. I looked in his eyes." She sets the pencil down and gives Polly a hard look.

Polly grimaces. "His guilt was proved. Proved in court."

Nell puts her hands on the table with a force that surprises Polly. "Look, Polly, you're a fine lawyer and there's no doubt about that, but a chipmunk could have had that boy convicted. It was his word against a white man's."

Polly feels his insides sink. He knows Nell disapproves of the sentence, has known it all along. But he needs her to believe in Willie's guilt. He looks pleadingly at his wife. She returns his gaze, unflinching.

"If he didn't rape her," Polly asks, grasping, "why would the girl have killed herself?"

Nell's expression softens into a mixture of disappointment and pity. "Think about it, Polly. The boy said he loved her. If she loved him, too—well, there wasn't going to be a good way out of any of it for either of them. Maybe it was more than she could bear."

"She could have testified on his behalf."

"Polly." Nell frowns. "If her father had even allowed it, what on earth kind of a life would she've been left with then?"

The kettle starts to howl. Nell stands, and Polly shuts his eyes. He hears the kettle's whistle fade, hears the cabinet open, the clink of china, first on the countertop, and a minute later on the table beneath him. He opens his eyes; dark liquid steams in a blue-rimmed mug.

Nell is looking down at him, her head tilted slightly to the side. She puts her hand on his shoulder, and when Polly lifts his hand to touch hers with his own, she takes it away and walks over to the screen door, where she stands with her back to the room. Laughter from outside floats inside: the Gildorfs' guests leaving, the party over. It is ten o'clock, and Polly is tired, but his evening has only just begun. He lifts the mug and drinks, and he hardly feels it when the boiling liquid scalds his tongue.

Nell

Nell stands at the screen door. She knows that Polly needs her now, but staying in the room is as much as she can do.

She hears him push his chair back from the table and lower the coffee mug into the sink, and in another moment she feels him touch her on the shoulder. She touches his hand, just briefly, and then his hand is gone. She listens to his footsteps leave the room, and soon she hears the front door close, the car engine choke to life, then fade as it drives away.

Still, Nell doesn't move from the doorway. She rests her head against the frame, exhausted yet unwilling to go to bed; she feels it her duty to wait until the thing, tonight, is done. She stands there, staring at the thin wires of the screen, so many tiny squares, and then adjusting her gaze to see through them, where outside leaves of butterfly ginger are wan in filtered streetlight, the broad fronds arcing beneath the delicate two-lobed blossoms. She can smell them, a rich, sweet scent. Coffee, too—she can smell that in the room behind her, where hangs still the lingering smell of grease.

Soon Nell hears footsteps somewhere outside; stiffening, she lifts her head from the door frame at the same time as she sees the priest emerge like a ghost from the shadows into which just hours ago he disappeared. He carries the basket that earlier had held Willie's food, and he looks about as weary as Nell feels. Maybe more.

"Father," Nell says, through the screen. She is both curious and at the same time unsurprised to see him here.

The man stands outside the door. He says nothing; though he is a grown man, he wears the hapless expression of a boy. "It's late, I know," he says. "I'm sorry."

Nell pushes the door open. "Come in," she says.

The priest obeys, and climbs the single step through the kitchen door, where he stops just inside, the basket hanging from a hand. Nell takes it from him and brings it to the counter, where she sees the remainder of the pie she'd made for Willie atop a stack of dishes. She hesitates, then takes the pie from the basket and, for now, sets it on the counter. She next unpacks the dishes, one by one, and sets them on the shelf.

"You washed them. You didn't need to do that."

"You didn't need to cook," the priest replies, behind her.

She turns around and regards him with a level gaze. "Maybe I did," she says. She takes a step toward him. "And aren't you meant to be with him, as he dies?"

The father nods. "I am. I plan to be."

"But here you are."

"Yes." She sees him swallow. "I needed to do something between now and then."

Nell doesn't pry. Instead she goes to the table and sits down at her drawing. "Sit," she says.

The priest pulls out a chair—the one where Polly sat minutes ago.

"My husband has to be there, too," Nell says, as Hannigan sits down. "He just left."

The priest looks at her, curious.

"As prosecuting DA," Nell goes on, "it's his duty to bear witness."

"I see." Hannigan frowns. "Your husband—" he begins, but Nell cuts him off.

"My husband is a good man," she says. "I want you to know that. I don't like what's happening tonight, and I know you don't, but I still swear my Polly is a good man. I won't get into things, but he was in a tough spot, a spot I wouldn't want to be in. Oh, God, and now this boy's going to die." She brings a hand to her mouth.

The woman and priest contemplate each other. Finally, Hannigan nods. He is sweating, and loosens his collar.

Nell lowers her hand to the table. "Can't imagine having to wear that garb in this heat," she comments, breaking the silence.

"It is warm," Hannigan agrees. "Though I sometimes feel, heat or no, I don't belong in it."

"It's garb to bear, I'd wager," Nell replies. "When in the end we're humans all."

Hannigan is quiet; he looks almost dumbfounded.

"I meant no disrespect—"

"No, no," the priest cuts her off. "None taken." His brow furrows. "You're not from here," he says. "The south."

Nell shakes her head. "No, I'm not. And it's been thirteen years but sometimes I still feel I don't belong in *this* garb." She gestures widely. "This place, this house, this town. For instance, tonight. Now."

"Yet you stay."

"Of course I stay. It's my life. The one I chose." She looks at him quizzically. "Why else do *you* stay?"

"Here?" Hannigan asks.

Nell shakes her head. "In the priesthood. If you feel like you don't belong. Isn't it because it's the life you chose?"

Hannigan takes a breath. "I came to the priesthood late. At that point in my life, I didn't know what else to choose."

"What point was that?"

Hannigan hesitates before he answers. "A dark point. It doesn't matter. Let's just say I'm as lost a soul as any."

"Maybe, but you're still able to guide other souls well enough, is what I've heard."

"Well I suppose that's what I live for. I suppose that's why I stay." He laughs. "The blind leading the blind." He looks at her. "What do *you* live for?"

Nell frowns. "I'm a mother," she says, glancing upward, gesturing toward Gabe's bedroom. "I suppose I care for many things, but what I live for is my boy."

Gabe

They take Amos Hicks's car. Amos drives, and the tall man sits shotgun. Buddy sits in the middle of the backseat, between his father and Gabe. The windows are down, but the breeze is about as refreshing as an electric dryer vent. Trees and fields flash by them in the darkness as they speed down an empty highway, all of them silent aside from Buddy, who starts to speak, but is hushed by a swat from his father.

After some time, the car slows down. Amos Hicks lowers his head to squint through the windshield, then turns onto a dirt road so bumpy that Gabe has to hold the door handle to keep himself in place. They lurch along through low scrub trees into wetland, the air dank with the scent of peat; Gabe breathes it in deeply, as if it were quenching a pulmonary thirst.

After a couple of miles, they reach a clearing at the edge of a large lake. Gabe can't see the water as much as he can sense the openness, the vast, dark expanse beyond the clearing. The car stops, and the familiar marshy smell is replaced by a sickening odor, sweetly rancid, overwhelming. Like death. Gabe pulls his shirt up over his nose and peers through the windshield, trying to figure out just where they are.

In the beam of the headlights, he can see a makeshift lean-to built against the trunk of a cypress tree, its limbs swathed in gray cascading curls of Spanish moss. Nearby, stumps have been arranged in a circle around an unlit fire pit, where empty beer bottles lie strewn in the dirt. A mirror hangs on the trunk of a second tree, and it is beneath this tree that Gabe locates the source of the smell.

It is hard, at first, for him to know what he is looking at; it looks like a table covered by some sort of cloth. But the cloth is red, meaty, dripping, not cloth at all, he understands, but the flesh of a carcass. A human, he thinks, and he thinks of black men hanging from trees, of Moses Beauparlant and Frix Mobley, who went missing last year when the FBI came into town and turned up dead a few weeks later. The tall man whistles. "One big fucking gator, he got," he says. Gabe blinks; a gator, of course.

"There's Pope," Amos says, gesturing out through the windshield as Pope Crowley emerges from the shadows on the other side of the lean-to. He is unshaven, shirtless beneath his suspenders. He dries his hands on his pants, then salutes into the beam of headlights, squinting as he ambles toward the car.

"Smell's gonna make me puke," Buddy mutters. His father jabs him quiet.

Pope leans into Amos's open window. "Thought y'all might of forgot where my camp was at," he says. His lower lip is fat with dip.

"Nah," Amos says. "Road's the worse for wear, though."

"The way I like it." Pope spits into the dirt, a brown river.

"Fine gator you got," the tall man says, leaning over in his seat toward the driver's side window.

Pope looks over his shoulder at what remains of the alligator. "Yeah. Got me that this afternoon. Just done skinning it."

"Reckon you should salt it?" the tall man asks. "Time you get back here may be too late."

"Pfff." Pope sticks his head back through the window, looks at the tall man dismissively. "I waited a day before between skinning and salting. And wouldn't miss this nigger fry for all the gator skins on God's green earth." He shifts his dip. "Can't imagine you would, neither."

"I'd have preferred to have killed him myself," the tall man responds, his words slow, fluid. Pope regards him, nods. Then his eyes travel to the backseat. "What all're they doing here?" he asks, of the boys. His gaze comes to rest on Gabe. "We got a problem with ol' Polly agin?"

"Apple falls far, turns out," Mr. Cunningham says. "Boy wanted to come 'long and see the show. Ol' man wouldn't take him."

"That right," Pope says. He stands up, spits again, then opens the car's back door, where Gabe is sitting. "Move it," he says, and Gabe slides across the seat as close to Buddy as he can.

Pope lowers himself into the car, and Gabe smells the punky blend of tobacco, beer, and body. Clammy nausea washes over him.

Amos Hicks turns the car around, and they bump back down the rutted lane to the state road. Once there, they drive straight and fast into the shaft of the headlights. Pope Crowley is humming, his bare skin slick against Gabe's arm. Gabe can feel his foot falling asleep, but he doesn't dare move it from the foot well, where it is wedged next to Pope's. He just stares out the windshield, trying not to think.

"Well look-y, look-y, look-y here!" Mr. Cunningham's voice is loud in the men's long silence. "Slow on down, Amos," Mr. Cunningham says, reaching forward to touch Amos on the shoulder.

Amos slows; a mule and wagon, pulled over on the edge of the road, gradually appear in the headlights. An old man sits on the lowered wagon bed, squinting into the lights. He stands, and raises his hand.

"Pull on over," Mr. Cunningham instructs.

"Let's just keep on," the tall man growls in the front. "Ain't got no time for this."

"Pull on over, Amos," Mr. Cunningham says again. "Let's see what's all up here."

Amos pulls off the road and stops the car a few yards behind the wagon. Mr. Cunningham opens his door, puts one foot on the ground before turning back inside. "You with me, Pope?" he asks.

Pope nods, and the two men climb out of the car.

Frank

He can see little in the beam of headlights, can't even tell what type of car has pulled over to the side of the road. He stands up from where he sits on the open tailgate and shields his eyes with a hand. One of the car doors opens, then another, and two figures emerge. They do not shut the doors behind them; these fan out from the car like wings. Frank watches the men approach, featureless in the blinding light. He doesn't pray as much as steels himself, wills this thing to go the way he needs it to.

The men stop a few feet from the wagon, regarding Frank. He can see their features more clearly, now: one has a lazy eye, and sucks on a load of dip; the other is stout and solid, eyes and nose small and close-set, burrowed in his face. Behind them, the car engine growls. Frank waits for them to speak.

"Well, Pope," the stout man says, finally. "What you reckon we have here?"

Pope spits a brown stream to the ground; it spatters just in front of Franks' feet. "Looks to me like a mule pulling its own stone to the grave," he says. He eyes the slab of granite in the back of the wagon thoughtfully, shifting the dip with his tongue.

"Looks to me like a pretty rich stone," the first man says. "Pretty rich stone for a nigger who can't afford a proper mule, anyway."

174

Pope looks from the stone to Frank. Or his right eye does. "What's yer story, old man?"

Frank wipes his brow with his forearm. Normally, he would give a simple answer, try to defuse the situation, but now it seems to him he doesn't have much to lose. "Mule sure is just about ready for the grave," he agrees. "But the stone for my son."

"Well, now," Pope says. "What I want to know is where a man like you got the money fer a stone like that."

"I borrowed it, sir," Frank says. "'Gainst all I have and more."

The first man's eyes narrow. "I don't know," he says, looking at Pope. "Now Pope, if you was you would you lend money to a nigger like him?"

Pope's right eye doesn't move from where he's fixed it on Frank. "Don't lend money to no one, but I'd be dead 'fore I did to the likes of him."

"Mmm-hmmm. Can't rightly imagine who would."

"Due respect, sirs, I got my slip right here." Frank takes the receipt the banker had given him that morning from his pocket and holds it out to the men. He watches his own hand shake, making the paper quiver, and suddenly he is overcome by the odd sensation that he is lifting from his body, rising upward like a ghost, or a helium balloon. He looks down at the self he's left behind, his thin, angled body, his glistening pate and trembling hand, the two solid men, the three of them lit bright and shimmering in the fumy headlights.

"Oh yeah?" he hears the stout man say, his voice distant, distorted. Frank sees him take the slip and rip it up without looking at it first. He tosses the fragments into the air, and

Frank watches the pieces rise up toward him and then flutter to the ground, white confetti in the headlights. "Who you trying to fool, nigger?" the stout man asks, as the scraps settle. Still as if from above, Frank sees the man reach out and cuff him on the shoulder, and with the blow he plunges back into his body, feels the ache, the heat.

He reaches for his shoulder and shakes his head, thinking how he's a fool in so many ways. A fool to have waited so long to get the stone, a fool to have taken the mule to get it, a fool to sit and wait for help when he should have known all the help he'd get would be the likes of this. "No one, sir," he mutters now. "Ain't trying to fool a soul, and don't want to trouble you no more." Nervously, he begins to collect the little pieces of receipt from where they have scattered on the ground. "I'm a fool myself. Y'all go on now. Don't mean to keep you, sure this time of night y'all have yer families to—" He stumbles sideways, blindsided by a shove. He falls to a knee, then catches himself, but as soon as he stands again he is shoved from the other side. Again, he stumbles, and this time he falls to his knees, and he doesn't get up. He lifts his hands. He keeps his eyes on the ground, which seems to glint and flicker, and his pulse thuds loudly in his brain. All other sounds are distant, his vision is dim, and then he shuts his eyes.

He kneels there in the heat, waits for the blows to come, the knee or toe to the underside of his chin, the hard strike of tire iron against his skull, whatever the worst can be. He finds himself thinking to Elma as if it were a prayer, *Elma, hear me, Elma,* sending her his love as the blood like love roars through his brain, and he can hear nothing else until that pulsing din is pierced by the shout of what can only be a child.

Frank opens his eyes. A figure stumbles into the headlights, a boy, his eyes wide, his red hair awry. "Stop it!" he shouts. "Let him alone!" The boy is out of breath, and his eyes dart frantically from one of the men to the other, though he does not look at Frank.

Frank's accosters look at the boy with a combination of surprise and disgust. For a second they are quiet, and then Pope spits. He snorts, and looks at the smaller man. "Apple falls far, you say, Walt, eh? Hah."

But Walt has already lunged toward the kid, grabbed him by the collar. "You mind your own goddamn business, you nigger-lovin' son of a whore!" He yanks the kid closer, fairly lifts him up by the collar. "You ain't no better than your daddy, and when I get through with you you gonna—"

"Walt." A third man has stepped into the lights, so tall that his features are hardly within the ring of illumination, and his voice seems disembodied. It is a low voice, firm. "Let the boy go, Walt. This ain't the evenin's business."

Walt flinches. Then he drops the boy's collar angrily.

"Like I said before," the tall man says. "We ain't got time for this."

"C'mon, Sutcliffe. We weren't gonna do nothing but rough him up a little," Pope says.

Sutcliffe looks at his watch. "Been waitin' on this too long to cut it close. Git in the car." He looks at Frank. "Stand up, man," he orders.

Frank stands, his hands still half raised above his head.

"And put yer damn hands down."

Frank lowers his hands slowly.

Sutcliffe looks at the other two men, and at the redheaded boy. "I said git in the car." He shakes his head. "Y'all just go lookin' for trouble," he mutters. He frowns, squinting down the highway into the distance, where a tiny speck of light is bouncing closer in from the horizon. The others follow his gaze, and when they, too, see the lights, they climb back into the car. Sutcliffe gets into the car last, lowering himself into the passenger seat, and the car accelerates abruptly away, wheels skidding on the gravel of the road. Frank shuts his eyes against the dust, stands there and listens: fading engine, growing engine, night bugs, his heart, and he keeps his eyes closed even as the light from the nearing car has turned the insides of his eyelids burning white.

Dale

He stares into the headlights, his hand draped over the wheel. Beside him, Ora sits upright, alert. "Up here," she says, after some minutes on the state road.

Dale peers out into the night; up ahead, he can see a car along the side of the road. He slows down while they're still a distance away, almost stops; as they watch, the car pulls abruptly into the road and speeds away. The taillights disappear beyond a billow of drifting dust.

"Well, go on," Ora says, gesturing ahead, where Dale can now see a mule and wagon along the road. A man is standing there, too, his arms at his sides.

"Ora," Dale says. "I don't know what this is about, but—"

"Dale," Ora interrupts. She glares at him. "You don't want to help, don't help. But don't you get in my way." She climbs out of the truck before he can respond, and he watches her run down the road. Her feet are bare, and her heels flash white in the headlights. He doesn't know what to think except his wife has gone crazy, and it makes the burden of his knowledge all the worse. If she's crazy now, he thinks.

Slowly, he pulls up behind the wagon and climbs out of the truck. He stops several feet away from where Ora and the man stand talking, crosses his arms. "This the man that needs our help?" he asks, looking at his wife.

"This is the man," Ora says.

"And what's the help?"

Ora nods at the mule and wagon. "Mule won't budge."

Dale looks at the mule and wagon, both equally rickety and run-down. "And how are we supposed to help with that?"

"Don't need help with the mule, sir," the man says. Dale looks at him. He is an older man, the bones of his face prominent beneath the wrinkled tapestry of his skin, and he's dressed in slacks and a button-down, which is opened at the collar and damp with sweat. His eyes look tired. The man points to the wagon bed. "Need help getting that where it needs to go."

Dale's eyes travel to where the man is pointing; next to a shovel and pick, a granite slab lies on the wooden planks. A tombstone.

"My boy's getting buried in the morning. I got to have his grave ready."

"Your boy," Dale repeats, his eyes on the tombstone.

"Killed in the war, Dale." This is Ora. "Serving his country same as anyone. Ain't that right." It is more of a statement than a question, a request for affirmation.

"Yes'm," the old man mutters.

It occurs to Dale that perhaps he's dreaming, that none of this is really happening.

"Where does it need to go?" He hears Ora say this; he has not lifted his eyes from the stone.

"Black cemetery, St. Martinville. Ain't far."

"No, it's not," Ora says. "We can help with that. Right? Dale?"

Dale stares at the stone. He hasn't thought about a tombstone, yet, or even considered where Tobe will be buried. He hasn't given thought to Tobe's body, and how they'll get it home. He doesn't even know what sort of a body is left, how bludgeoned, how maimed. He realizes that he hasn't thought about much of anything beyond telling Ora; all of a sudden he sees clearly how very much there still is to go through.

"Right, Dale?" Ora asks again.

Dale clears his throat. "Yuh," he says. "I suppose."

Frank

The man wordlessly helps him move the stone from the wagon into the truck bed. It is not heavy as much as awkward in its size to maneuver; they slide it off the wagon bed, then each holds an end as they carry it to the truck. The woman shadows them with the pick and shovel, which she slides onto the truck bed beside the stone, and also a rifle. Frank's eyes linger on the rifle, then he shifts his gaze to the man. "That loaded?" he asks.

The man looks at Frank, and then over at the mule. Bess stands with her head low. Her eyes look glazed, and she is foaming at the mouth. She's hardly more than a coated skeleton. The man blinks, then reaches for the rifle and hands it to Frank.

Frank nods his thanks, brings the rifle over to the wagon, and props it on its butt against the wagon wheel. He goes around the front to Bess, cups her soft ears with his hands. She hardly seems to notice he is there; Frank breathes deeply at this final confirmation. It is time. He unhooks her from the harness and bridle, takes the bit from between her lips, and with the rifle in one hand he gently guides her a few weary steps into the field. She stands there blinking. Frank places his hand against the white star on her forehead, slowly draws his hand down her nose. Then he steps back, lifts the rifle, and shoots the mule between her eyes.

She falls immediately. For a moment, Frank watches the blood seep from her wound. Then he crouches down beside her and lays a hand on her side; she is gone.

PART THREE

PART THREE

Lane

I t doesn't take long to drive the twelve miles to St. Martin-ville from New Iberia. The main road leads them to the center of town, where the parish courthouse stands in a dry expanse of lawn. A grand white building with a triangular roof, it has an overhang supported by large scrolled columns. The jail stands behind it.

They park on the street, and Lane cuts the engine. Seward takes a sip from his flask and opens the truck door, then slides himself to the ground. Lane stays in the driver's seat, hands on the steering wheel, staring at the branches of a tree outside. He can smell the woman on his hands, and her vanilla scent also wafts up from his chest, where her sweat mingled with his. He wishes he could shower.

Soon he hears the captain yell for him; he slides out of the truck and goes around to the back. Seward has opened the trailer, and is readying himself to climb inside. "Let's do this," he says.

As the two wrestle the chair to the ground, a crowd starts to gather. Men stand muttering in small groups near the jail, a handful of children, too, up late for the occasion. Some have climbed into the tree directly overhead, knocking acorns loose in their ascent. They squat in the branches like little monkeys, transfixed. Their presence makes Lane edgy, as complicit in this endeavor as the other men involved.

Two deputies from the St. Martinville jail stand by uselessly as Lane and the captain set the chair on the ground. Seward turns to them, wiping his forehead with the back of his arm. He is sweating copiously, nearly wheezing, and Lane wonders if the man might keel over. "All right," the captain says. "Where's this baby go?"

One of the deputies gestures over his shoulder toward the jail. "In there," he says. "Second floor."

Seward looks at the deputies with distaste. "My back ain't fit fer the task," he says, motioning the two men toward the chair. "I'll carry the wires."

Lane and the deputies lift the chair awkwardly. They tilt the whole thing back and struggle with it to the entrance of the jail, each deputy bearing a leg, and Lane the seat back. The death mask stares at him grimly.

It takes a few attempts to maneuver the chair through the jail doorway. Seward barks orders, curses. He has lit a cigar, and Lane finds the smoke nauseating. He grits his teeth, his skin slick, his body pulsing with heat. He feels weak from lack of food, and wishes he'd had more to eat, yet when he thinks of the jerky in his pocket, he retches. A man will soon be killed in this chair. He does not want to think of it, but even when he tries to turn his mind to the task at hand, the thought is there. A man will soon be killed in this chair.

On the third attempt, they get the chair through the doorway. Lane and the deputies set the chair down at the bottom of a narrow staircase, where they rest for a moment as the captain climbs up the steps ahead of them, carrying a coil of wires over his arm. Because of his limp, he takes the stairs like a young child, leading with the right foot, following with the left, his shirt back stained thoroughly with sweat.

In a moment, according to some unspoken cue, the three men lift the chair again and carry it clumsily up the stairs. The staircase turns three times, and each time the legs get caught, or the seat back hits the wall. "Back left room," one of the deputies pants, at the top of the stairs, and the men carry the chair down the hallway, past three cell doors with tiny barred windows. Lane can't see through them, but he has the distinct impression that there are prisoners inside, watching them, staring out.

The room designated for the execution is small and cramped, about double the size of Lane's cell back at Angola, which he can cross in three strides. It is lit dimly by an overhead light, in which Lane can see the shadows of dead flies caught by the celluloid covering. Seward is at the back of the room, his upper half out the window; at the sound of their entrance, he pulls himself inside. To Lane's relief, the cigar has gone out. "Set it here," the captain orders, pointing with the butt of the cigar. "Back to the window. That way we kin run the wires out to the truck."

Lane and the deputies set the chair as instructed. "All right," Seward says. He ties the ends of the wires to an arm of the chair and tosses the coil out the window, where the black cables unspool to the ground. "Let's hook 'er up," he says. He looks at Lane. "Come on, trusty."

Lane follows the captain back out to the truck. There's still an hour until midnight, but the crowd around the jail has gotten large. Lane observes the gathered people; earlier they were quiet and staring, but now they are talking loudly, giving only half their attention to the ghastly entertainment.

"Wait here," Seward says, when they have reached the truck. He takes a pull of his whiskey and hauls himself with great effort up into the trailer. Inside, he turns around. "Give me them wires," he orders.

Lane collects the ends of the cables from where they have tumbled to the ground. He hands them to Seward, who takes them deep inside the trailer, to the generator in the back. Soon, he emerges again, and lowers to the ground a green steel switchboard with several needle dials across the front. "Generator's connected," the captain reports. "Now I'm a take that up and connect the other end." He sits down on the trailer floor and slides to the ground. "When I say OK, you fire her up, see how she runs."

"Sir?"

"Red button on the side. Even a fool like you kin figure it out."

Seward lifts the switchboard and takes it toward the jail. Slowly, Lane climbs into the trailer, which seems much larger without the chair inside. He walks back to the generator and sits down beside it in the dark, waiting for the captain's cue. He looks out through the trailer's doorway, which frames the crowd; the children in the trees; and the cables, running like deadly snakes across the dirt and up through the jailhouse window.

Polly

He drives north out of town. The highway that leads to St. Martinville runs generally parallel to Bayou Teche, though if Polly didn't know it, he'd never guess there was a wide and slowly swirling waterway a few hundred yards away. He drives quickly, staring thoughtless and transfixed at the gray ribbon of concrete passing beneath his hood, and he's unsure, when he arrives at St. Martinville some twenty minutes later, whether the drive has felt more like seconds or hours.

Polly leaves his car several blocks away from the courthouse and approaches on foot, wanting to move. There are others walking in the same direction; one or two of them at first, then more and more as they converge on the square and finally join a swelling crowd, which has spilled from the courthouse green and all around the jail into the streets.

Polly pauses across the way. He takes his hat off, wipes the perspiration from his brow. Before him, the horde seems a single living thing: murmuring, shifting, breathing. He notices a small child at the edge of the crowd, attached to her father's hand, being pulled in, swallowed up. He imagines what it must be like from her vantage point: the legs and skirts and belt buckles, the courthouse lights shining down through the trees, the volleying voices over her head.

Polly wonders if the little girl is afraid. He thinks of Gabe's question earlier tonight—Does it hurt?—and then thinks of the sudden leap and thud, the gooseflesh and swell, the slump and wafting smoke, the things for which tonight he is responsible.

Willie

The sedan that will take him to the execution waits at the curb, its engine running. Willie stands at the top of the courthouse steps, handcuffed and shackled, Grazer on one side and another deputy on the other. His fresh clothes are stiff and have a smell that makes the back of his throat tickle.

It is late, dark, quiet. There is no blinding sunlight, no shouting; there are no hats or flashbulbs, as when Willie left the building to go to trial months ago. It is just him and the officers, the car and driver, and between them, Lady Justice, rising as she always does from the center of the staircase.

"Let's go," Grazer says, nudging Willie with his elbow. Willie looks down at his shackled legs as he descends the stairs, one small step at a time. It's an old man's shuffle, awkward, and it takes the three men some minutes to reach the sidewalk where the car is waiting. The deputy opens the door and slides in across the black leather of the seats. Grazer gestures to Willie to get in next. Willie turns first, and looks up for a final time at the small window of his fourth-floor cell. His heart races.

"Go on," Grazer says, prodding him.

Willie ducks into the car, pulls his legs in, and scoots across the seat. The only place to rest his feet is on the hump of the covered axle shaft, and his knees jut up nearly to his face.

Grazer lowers himself heavily into the seat beside Willie and slams the door. "You all right?" he asks.

Willie nods once. His ears are ringing. His mouth is dry.

They pull away from the curb and soon turn onto Main Street. Shadows sweep through the car as it passes beneath each streetlamp, arc after arc of tinny light. The storefronts are dark, the parking spots between the diagonal stripes on the pavement empty. Only a bakery shows any sign of life; steam rises from a round aluminum vent on the roof. Willie imagines the smell: fresh bread, cakes, vanilla, pastries—and it makes him think, fleetingly, of Grace. He shuts his eyes.

He doesn't open them for some time. He listens instead to the gravel of the highway strike the bottom of the car, and he thinks of rain. He tries to remember the last time he heard rain, but he can't summon the memory. Had he known at the time it was the last rain he'd ever hear, he'd have paid attention.

Beside him, Grazer begins to make a clicking sound at the back of his throat, and Willie can feel against his thigh the vibrations running through Grazer's own as he jiggles his foot. Willie opens his eyes and looks at the sheriff, at his dark profile against the night sky outside. "I be OK, sheriff," Willie tells him.

The sheriff's foot goes still as he turns to look at Willie. He looks as if he is going to say something, but he doesn't. Instead he blinks rapidly, then turns his face out toward the night.

Willie lets his gaze on the sheriff soften and focuses instead on the passing roadside fields beyond the man, the blue fields of sugarcane that used to terrify him. When he was a child, daytime warnings became nightmares, and he'd dream of being chased naked through the slashing stalks, his flesh being sliced into so many raw, red lines as he fled a white man. He can't remember who first told him that story, but he thinks now that this kind of fear never did anyone any kind of good.

Father Hannigan

The Joneses' house is in St. Martinville, just a half mile away from the courthouse where Willie will be executed. Hannigan pulls up outside and shuts the car engine off. The house stands in the moonlight, a clapboard shotgun with peeling white paint and a small front porch, a handful of steps leading down to the yard. He thinks of Nell, hears her words echo in his mind: *I suppose what I live for is my boy.*

He has been here once before, months ago, at a time when the execution was far enough away that it didn't seem real, or seemed somehow avoidable, something that might never come to be. Elma Jones had answered the door, that once. Hannigan could see Willie clearly in her features—warm dark eyes, broad nose, thin lips—though unlike Willie she was amply sized: solid, wide, and strong. Frank Jones had been in the back, hammering at something. Elma had called to him, and the old man had emerged slowly, nodding, wiping off his hands. When the three sat down to talk, Hannigan found that everything he'd prepared to say seemed inadequate, fitting for parents in the abstract; but here these people were, in front of him, parents in the flesh whose suffering he could little soothe. So together they had sipped tea, and he'd offered what he could: Prayer. Hope.

Hannigan looks at the house now; the windows are mostly dark, though he can see through one a dim glow. He steels himself and gets out of the car, takes the three steps up to the front porch in a single stride. The porch boards creak under his weight. He lifts a hand, hesitates, knocks.

In the distance, he thinks he can hear the mob he saw assembled outside the courthouse. It could also be the chattering of insects, or the noise of his own swarming mind. A breeze stirs, the movement of air stagnant for months, it seems. Hannigan turns. On the sidewalk behind him, a cellophane wrapper skitters, comes to rest; the leaves on the nearby tree move, just perceptibly, then are still. Hannigan waits, watching, and after a moment he turns and knocks on the door again.

He hears movement within, he is sure. He tips his head toward the door, listening. "Mr. Jones?" he calls softly, his face against the door frame. "Mrs. Jones?" He waits, hopeful, nearly aching. He wants to offer them more than promises and prayer; he wants to give them what is real: assurance that their boy is a fine, fine man.

When it is clear to him that no one is going to open the door, Hannigan takes the steps down to the curb. He turns to look back, and sees a figure standing at the window. Elma Jones. She does not duck out of sight or pull away when she sees that he has seen her. Instead, she gives him a slow nod of her head. After a moment, Hannigan presses his palms together before him and lowers his own head, his offering accepted, his duty done. When he looks up again, she is gone. He stares at the place where she was, half wondering if he'd made the vision up, to fill a personal need.

He gets into the car, but he doesn't drive away. He doesn't even turn the key in the ignition. Instead he sits with his hands on the wheel, and when he shuts his eyes he sees Elma Jones again, a shadowy figure behind the window glass. But then in his mind that shadowy figure starts to change—it is Elma Jones, it is Della Biggs, it is Nell, it is his own mother: scallions, songs, a red cotton blouse.

He holds on to that image: a woman in the shadows, his mother. He holds it there in his mind, studies it closely, searching. He can see a hand. He peers closer, willing himself to see, and slowly his mother's features come into focus—her eyes like gibbous moons, her lips a pale thin line, her hair dark and long and loose—this forgotten face so deeply familiar, yet seen as if for the first time.

He opens his eyes. His hands are still on the wheel, gripping it hard now. He stares absently at the ridges of his own knuckles, and he can still see her, his mother, her face, her hair, can smell and hear her, and as he sits there, he comes to understand that she did not kill herself, after his brother died. She did not kill herself; she left.

Hannigan blinks. He is less shocked or saddened than affirmed by this knowledge, unearthed from a corner of his mind he didn't know existed. He wonders what else is in there, and if he even wants to know. He looks back at the house, at the window where Elma Jones stood. Then he starts the car; there is less than an hour until midnight, and Willie will be waiting for him.

Gabe

They drive in silence. Gabe sits wedged in the backseat between Buddy and Pope, his breathing shallow with nerves. He thinks he has never felt such heat, from the outside in, leg to leg, arm to arm in an airless car on an airless night, but also from the inside out, radiating from his terrified core. He doesn't dare turn his head to look at either Pope or Mr. Cunningham. What had Gabe been thinking, running out to defend that old man? He can't explain it even to himself. He was in the car, watching through the windshield, and then he wasn't, he was overtaken, and he was out in the headlights, yelling. His heart is still pounding.

He watches the men in the front seats, Amos Hicks and Sutcliffe, but he can't tell from what he can see of them—cheekbones, temples, ears—what expressions they are wearing. Caliber's voice rings in Gabe's ear—*Grace Sutcliffe, baker's daughter*—but he is too afraid to ask, too afraid to wonder. He looks between the men and out through the windshield, where he sees only dirt and gravel; what he doesn't know is what's ahead. He thinks again of Frix Mobley, whose body was found out at the salt mines, dusted white; and Moses Beauparlant, whose body they found inside one of the old kilns. His stomach flips; he does not want to die. He stares, tense and alert, and his eyes play tricks on him; he sees ghostly mounds of salt in the shadows, the rubble of wrecked kilns.

He should have listened to his father, he knows. He should have stayed home, but he didn't and now here he is, exactly where he shouldn't be, squeezed again as he was months ago in the backseat of a car beside Pope Crowley.

In the front, Amos Hicks takes a long breath, clears his throat as he shifts in his seat. "Seems farther away than it is," he comments as the car slows down at an intersection. Up ahead, Gabe can just make out a smattering of lights, and he is flooded with relief. Amos looks at the tall man in the passenger seat, whose head grazes the felt of the ceiling. "But we made it on time to your show, Sutcliffe."

"Mmmmm," Sutcliffe mutters, as the car speeds up again.

"We here?" asks Buddy.

"Just about," Amos answers.

At this, Gabe sits back, lets his shoulders drop. He has never been so grateful to arrive at a place. They are here. They are here, here to watch a man be killed, but Gabe is thankful. He is being spared.

Nell

S he is not asleep, not really. Part of her is sleeping, surely, drifting along just beneath the level of consciousness, but a corner of her mind is awake, is aware of the sound of the dripping sink, of an itch on her knee, of the tabletop warm against her cheek, of the fact that another part of her mind is dreaming. She floats in that in-between realm, willing neither to pull herself completely into wakefulness nor to capitulate entirely to sleep. Instead, she hovers, and it is snowing. She is outside and looking up at a black sky, at fat flakes of snow coming down as hard and fast as they seem to fly at you through the windshield when you drive into a storm. And then she isn't standing outside anymore; instead she actually *is* driving through the storm. And then the flakes change from snow into stars, the car is gone, and she is speeding untethered through the universe.

It is a strange half dream, born of delirious exhaustion, and for some time she allows herself to linger there, even as the sink drips, even as her cheek is going numb against the table. She lets herself drift through snow, through stars, and then in the distance she sees their own home, the one that she is in now, but instead of being in a town, it stands alone in a dark field. And she can see the lit kitchen window—the only source of light—can see herself through it, a figure slumped over the table, and she drifts close, closer, until finally she merges with herself.

She opens her eyes, looks at the kitchen sideways. She doesn't sit up immediately, but instead lets herself ease back into the night, the present. She moves her fingers first, then her toes, blinks her eyes clear. She is suddenly aware of being hot, extremely hot, and thinks it interesting that unlike the dripping of the water or the itch on her knee, the overwhelming heat did not follow her into her dream. It makes her wonder what might not have followed her out. She remembers snow, stars, the house, herself, but there could have been something else, something important, which, now that she is awake, is as absent from wakefulness as the stifling heat was from her dream. She can make no sense of the snow, of the stars, of anything she remembers, and she feels increasingly certain that the heart of the dream, its meaning, may have been left behind.

She frowns and lifts her head from the table. The clock reads eleven twenty-eight, and her chest opens with dread. She stands and goes to the sink for a glass of water, which she drinks looking out the window above the faucet. Their backyard comes up against the yard of the house on the next street south, and Nell can see through the gaps in the dividing hedge the kitchen of the Goodsons, their elderly neighbors. The light is on, and Mr. and Mrs. Goodson sit at their kitchen table, a portable radio between them. Nell can guess what they are listening to; they are never up so late. But there they are, near midnight, holding hands across the kitchen table. They don't look at each other; Nell thinks that perhaps they can't.

She looks away from the Goodsons, allows her eyes to drift to the portable radio on her own counter. She reaches toward it, and after a moment's hesitation, she turns it on.

It doesn't take her long to find the station she is looking for, the chattering voices narrating the evening's grim affair.

"Time is rapidly running out for Willie Jones," a voice says. "Over by the jail, they've already opened up the truck, it's all ready to go, all set so that the juice will be funneled up through these cables to the chair."

"That's right, Joe. The truck's ready to go, and the prisoner is about to arrive, and it won't take long to prep him, strap him down . . ."

"And perform his last rites, right, Bob?"

"That's right, I believe those are available should the prisoner wish to—"

Nell snaps the radio off. She doesn't want to hear any more.

Frank

F rank stares into the night, willing the lights of St. Martinville to appear in the distance. The man sits silently in
the driver's seat beside him, wearing the same hard expression
he's been wearing since he first appeared tonight. His wife
sits in the truck bed, even though Frank had already climbed
up there himself when they were ready to go. But the woman
insisted that he ride inside the cab—so that he could direct
them more easily to the cemetery, she'd said. And so she sits
with the tombstone, her back against the cab window, watching the road behind them disappear into the night.

Frank looks at the clock on the dashboard: eleven-thirty.
It was later than he'd thought it was when he climbed into
the truck, a good deal later; now every time he checks the
clock desperation courses through his body. The promise
of seeing his son one last time has today been sustenance
to Frank, has kept at bay thoughts of tomorrow, thoughts
of the future, when Willie is gone. *Now,* Willie is alive. *Still,*
Willie is alive. Frank still can tell himself that he will see his
son again, and this has been a comfort whose magnitude
he hadn't recognized until now.

The man's voice breaks the silence. "Sorry about your boy."

Frank glances over at the man. He does not know how
to respond, and so he simply nods once to acknowledge the
condolence. "Sir," he mumbles.

"Where was he stationed?" The man asks this without taking his eyes off the road.

Frank swallows. He has never been one to be untruthful, but the lie came so easily when the woman asked him how his son had died. It makes him feel uneasy to have blamed the war, as if in saying this he will have made it true, and now he will lose Darryl, too. But what else was he to say? He brings a hand to his face and with forefinger and thumb rubs his eyes.

"Sorry," he hears the man say. "Understand if you don't want to talk."

Frank lowers his hand and looks over at the man, whose eyes dart back and forth between Frank and the road ahead. Frank nods. "Obliged," he says. "For everything."

The man returns his gaze exclusively to the road, where, when Frank follows suit, he sees St. Martinville up ahead. Frank shuts his eyes in thanks.

"Show me which way to go up here," the man says.

The cemetery is on the north side of town, not far from the river, but Frank says nothing as they drive past the street they'd need to take to get there. "This way," he says, a minute later, and points to a street that leads in the opposite direction.

Gabe

Mr. Cunningham steers both Gabe and Buddy through the crowd by their necks. The other three men walk up ahead, pushing through the throng. The close press of bodies, the stink and heat, the din of voices—it's all dizzying. But Gabe walks obediently where Mr. Cunningham directs him; he understands that he doesn't have a choice.

Pope and the other two men stop in the far corner of the green, beneath the limbs of a water oak. Gabe looks up at the broad branches. A gallows, yes, but also an escape. He tries to shrug himself out from beneath Mr. Cunningham's hand, but his movement only makes the man's grip tighten around his neck. Gabe twists his head up in surprise; Mr. Cunningham squints down at him suspiciously. "Just where you think you're going, boy?"

"Nowhere, sir. I mean, I thought I'd climb the tree, if that's OK, sir."

Mr. Cunningham looks from Gabe to the tree above them. Then he releases his grip, half shoving Gabe forward as he does.

Gabe hoists himself up into the branches. He scrapes his knee against the rough bark as he climbs, but he hardly notices, grateful to be out of the crowd, away from his companions.

From above, the mob of spectators seems like an odd pattern of heads and shoulders, shadows and artificial light from the streetlamps circling the green. It is larger than any crowd Gabe has seen before. The sidewalk near the jail has been cordoned off, and deputies stand guard. Nearby, Gabe can see a truck parked in the street, its back open, wires snaking out and up the side of the building, and Gabe understands that these will zap the life out of Willie Jones. He follows the wires in his imagination through the window and into that second-floor room, where he can see the deadly chair, the straps and buckles, a cloaked executioner, smoke and sparks. His father, too. *Got that nigger just what he deserves.*

Suddenly, the chatter of voices rises; heads begin to turn in one direction. Gabe looks that way, too, and sees a black car approaching from down the street, moving slowly as the people in the street give way. They do so solemnly, almost respectfully, it seems to Gabe, even though they're here to see the man inside die.

The car pulls up against the curb outside the jail, and the back door opens. A deputy climbs out first, followed by Willie Jones. He is tall, thin, his head shaved bare. His hands and ankles are bound together, and his posture is one of weary defeat, his head lowered, his shoulders limp. A big man climbs out of the car last, after Willie. He wears a uniform of navy blue, someone more powerful than an ordinary deputy. This man puts a hand on the small of Willie's back and begins to steer him across the sidewalk.

There is a commotion, then, as the deputies lining the barrier converge around a man who has stepped onto the sidewalk into Willie's path. The big man in the uniform drops his hand from Willie's back and steps forward, gestures the deputies back to their places with angry motions of his hands;

they obey. The man stands where he was, unmoving in the middle of the sidewalk, where Willie has also stopped. The man is built like Willie, but thinner, older; there is no doubt in Gabe's mind that he is Willie's father.

The man steps forward and takes Willie in his arms, holding Willie's bald skull in the palm of his hand, his long fingers spread wide around Willie's scalp. Willie's face rests against the old man's shoulder. How familiar to each other they must be, Gabe thinks—that skull the same one the old man cupped his hand around when Willie was a baby, the crevice between the older man's neck and shoulder the same one Willie wept on as a boy. Gabe thinks of his own father's shoulder, the ledge of collarbone, the cedar scent of his shaving cream, the crisp fabric of his shirt, and he feels his throat tighten. He shuts his eyes. He doesn't want to be here. He doesn't want to see. He would give anything, he thinks, to stop this thing from happening.

Willie

He breathes deeply of his father's skin, the valley between his eyes filled precisely by the muscle of the old man's shoulder, a perfect fit. He feels his father's fingers against his skull, each one a reassuring point of pressure holding Willie close, pulling him in. He surrenders, lets himself be held, as awkward as the pose is with his shackled hands between them. In his father's arms, everything falls away—the heat, the hundreds of people around them, the waiting chair, his fate. For the first time since he was accused, he feels safe, and he presses his head more into his father's shoulder, presses it hard, with all the weight of his love.

Ora

They sit in the truck in silence, parked on a side street in St. Martinville. Every few minutes, people pass by them on the sidewalk in the direction where Frank had headed. He'd said only that he had to tell his boy good-bye, and Ora had promised that they'd wait. To her surprise, Dale didn't argue. He didn't say anything at all, still hasn't said anything. He's said nothing about where they are, or who Frank is, though by now they know.

Ora sits very still in the seat where Frank sat moments ago, her hands clasped tightly in her lap. Every now and then she glances at Dale sideways; he looks as fierce as she feels, his eyes fixed forward as he works his jaw, his eyes bright. She wants to speak to him, but doesn't know what to say.

It isn't long before Ora sees Frank returning. He walks quickly, though with a tired limp, his head low. Instead of getting into the back with the stone again, Ora slides over into the middle of the front seat to ride between the two men. Dale's leg stiffens when her thigh presses up against his, as if the feel of her were poison. The feel of him has the opposite effect on her; the familiarity of it is devastating, and she is overcome by a sudden urge to weep.

Frank gets into the truck wordlessly. He is dry-eyed, but Ora can see that his hands are shaking. She thinks to reach for one of them, to take his hand in hers, but something stops her. Frank pulls the truck door closed behind him, and Dale turns on the engine.

"All right," Dale says. To Ora's surprise, his tone is less angry than defeated, and she looks over at him. He's got both hands on the steering wheel, his grip so tight that the skin stretches white over the knob of every knuckle. He takes a deep breath and looks at Frank. He nods once, and says, "Point the way."

Polly

P olly waits in the execution room with the five other witnesses for Captain Seward to return. The room is small,
hot, uncomfortable; Polly has removed his jacket and loosened
his tie, yet his shirt clings to the small of his back, and he can
feel perspiration seeping through his every pore.

The chair sits against the room's south wall. Looms there,
making the space feel even smaller than it is. The seat waits
as if with an open lap, the leather straps and buckles that will
hold Willie down dangling off to either side. At the top of the
chair there is a crown of metal and gauze, and draped over
the back, a leather gag. Gruesome Gertie indeed. Twenty-two
men have died in its arms. A woman, too, who had wept when
she learned that her head would have to be shaved.

The witnesses stand in silence, none able to hold another's gaze. Through the open window, they can hear the
crowd. Finally, there is a rumbling outside that erupts into
a deafening roar. The generator. Polly checks his watch; it is
four minutes until midnight.

Seward comes back into the room, breathing heavily.
His face is red, and he emanates a rank scent made worse by
the closeness of the room: filth, tobacco, whiskey, sweat, as
if the man has not showered in weeks. Willie Jones comes in
behind him, followed by Sheriff Grazer and Sheriff Roselle,
of St. Martinville. Polly nods at Grazer, but Grazer does not

notice. His face is hard, expressionless, though his mouth seems to twitch as he gestures Willie over toward the chair.

Willie obeys, his face as bewildered as it has always seemed to be to Polly. He sits down on the hard seat of the chair, watching as Sheriff Grazer removes his cuffs and shackles. Then the sheriff stands, nods at the prisoner, and steps back to allow the deputies to begin the work of strapping Willie in.

Seward mutters orders that Polly cannot make out over the din of the generator. He finds himself therefore watching with clinical detachment. A necessary detachment. The deputies strap Willie's biceps to his sides, and then to the back of the chair. They strap his wrists tightly to the chair's arms. Another thick strap goes around his waist, and several others around his thighs and calves. One of the deputies rips open Willie's pants leg and attaches an electrode to his calf. Through all of this, Willie sits very still, passive and unresisting, though his eyes rove in what must be fear.

When the deputies have finished, Sheriff Roselle steps forward to read the state of Louisiana's death decree. "Now, therefore, I, James Davis, Governor of the State of Louisiana, do hereby direct and require you, the Sheriff of the Parish of St. Martin, to cause the execution to be done on the body of said Willie Jones so convicted and condemned, in all things according to the judgment and sentence of said Court and the law in all such cases made and provided, by electrocution, that is, causing to pass through the body of said Willie Jones a current of electricity of sufficient intensity to cause death, and the application and continuance of such current through the body of the said Willie Jones, until said Willie Jones is dead."

Polly knows these words by heart, so often has he looked at them since Willie's sentence was pronounced.

Sheriff Roselle steps back, and the priest in the room steps forward. He kneels down and puts both of his hands atop Willie's, and then he lowers his head so that his forehead rests against Willie's knee. After a moment, the priest stands. He touches Willie's head, then retreats to the far wall, his face stricken. Polly wonders if this is the same priest who took his wife to see the boy the other day. *The boy.* He breathes deeply, swallows hard as if to swallow the panic he feels rising from within.

He looks from the priest to Willie just at the moment Seward pulls a thick black hood over Willie's face; Polly sees him flinch as the hood comes down. Then one deputy tightens the metal crown around Willie's head while another gags his mouth, strapping the gag to the back of the chair so roughly that Willie's head bangs audibly against the wood.

Willie

I t hurts him, but he doesn't care. The sudden darkness
is a relief, after all the buzzing around him, the buck-
ling and strapping and fastening and clipping, after the
sickening way the folks there watching seemed to be in
a big swing, swinging away from him and then right up
close so that he could almost hear them breathing. He sits
in the darkness, feeling his pulse slow, his breathing even
out. He is sweating, but at the same time he feels cold. A
spot on his leg begins to itch, but he cannot move his arm
to scratch it. This is what he thinks about in the darkness:
the itch on his leg. The itch on his leg; in the darkness,
there is nothing else.

   And then: a million needles and pins start to puncture
his skin, everywhere on his body—a sensation he doesn't
immediately understand. He imagines the deputies with
pins attached to every finger, poking at him, or maybe bat-
tering him with paddles studded with needles. He tries to
call out, but he cannot get his tongue to work; it is like a
lead ball in his mouth, immovable and cold. And then in
the darkness there appear flecks of light, blue and green and
pink speckles, and he thinks they must be poking the hood
now, too, and it reminds him of the night sky, the stars like
little holes, specks of light like these that flood his vision

now, bursting and sputtering as the needles batter the hood, batter his skin, driving harder and deeper until he hears his own cry echo in his head and he understands at last that this is it, that finally he is dying.

Father Hannigan

After the captain throws the switch, at first the only thing that happens is that Willie's hands—the long, cold fingers, all those slender bones—clench into tight fists. Or maybe other things happen, too, but this is what Hannigan looks at: Willie's fists. Only when he hears Willie groan does Hannigan look for the boy's face, covered in its awful hood. There is a mouth slit in the hood; the pink flesh of Willie's lips puffs out, so grossly have they swelled. Next the boy's body begins to strain and writhe, so violently that the enormous chair lurches across the floor, propelled by the force of Willie's convulsions. Hannigan watches in horror.

Then, just as quickly as it started, the current stops. Willie's thrashing body slumps. The witnesses are quiet. Seward stands up from where he'd crouched down over the electrical panel. He is breathing heavily through his nose with what seems to Hannigan perverse satisfaction. The parish coroner and his assistant step forward to examine Willie's body. Hannigan shuts his eyes. He thinks of Willie's lips; he doesn't want to see what might have happened to the rest of the boy's face.

Eyes closed, Hannigan is aware that he is trembling. Surely, he thinks, in a world where such a thing as this exists, surely there can be no God. And yet despite this thought, he finds that he is praying anyway—not a prayer of words, not a plea to any God, but a prayer of focused feeling. He keeps his eyes closed and concentrates. It is all that he can do.

"He's breathing," he hears, in a moment. Voices gasp and mutter. Hannigan opens his eyes.

"Well damn it, we'll give him another one!" the executioner sputters angrily, and before anyone can stop him or say otherwise, he flips the switch again, and again, Willie's body starts to convulse, just as it did before. Hannigan holds his fists to his temples, forcing himself to watch what Willie is being forced to endure. "Give me more juice down there!" the executioner shouts angrily out the window. "More juice, damn it!"

But nothing changes; Willie's body jerks and writhes against the restraints, the chair skitters, the gag comes loose, smoke rises from the cables where they connect to the back of the chair, and then, all of a sudden, Willie gasps, a desperate, strangled suck of air, and stutters through his torture, "*I am not dying!*"

Sheriff Grazer steps forward at this, strides across the floor toward the chair. "Turn it off, man!" he yells at the executioner. Seward turns the switch, and again Willie's body slumps into the chair. A few seconds later, the generator shuts down, and the room is quiet.

Polly

Wordlessly, the deputies unstrap Willie from the chair and peel the electrodes from his skin. One pulls the hood from his face; Willie blinks at the sudden light, gasping for breath. His lips are oozing, and strands of drool stretch between them. Polly watches the deputies flit around him, unbuckling and unbinding, revealing swaths of scorched skin. He feels oddly calm, collected, resolved, as if something nebulous inside him has crystallized.

"Bloody hell," Seward curses. He jabs a finger in Willie's direction. "I'm going to go fix that generator and I'm coming right back, and if the electricty doesn't kill you this time, well then I'm gonna kill you with a rock." He slams his fist into his hand and leaves the room, knocking the chair with his hip as he passes it.

Sheriff Grazer takes Willie by the arm and helps him out of the chair; Willie takes a few unsteady steps forward, his body shaking. "Am I dead?" he's asking. "What's happening? Am I dead?"

"Take him back to the holding room," Sheriff Roselle instructs. "Lay him down on the cot in there."

The remaining witnesses watch Willie go, Sheriff Grazer's arm around his waist. Even after the two are gone, the others in the room stand in stunned silence. The coroner's assistant, a very young man, is quietly weeping; Polly puts a hand on his thin shoulder.

"What does one do, in a situation like this?" It is the coroner who breaks the silence.

"Never been a situation like this," Roselle says, gruffly. He sniffs. "I reckon if that fool can get the chair fixed right we'll try it again."

Polly's mind races, and he can feel a peculiar energy gathering inside him; it is a familiar sensation, one he used to get all the time when arguing a case in court.

"It doesn't seem right," he hears the priest say.

"Jones was sentenced to die on a specific date. It's our duty to fulfill that order," Roselle says. "This been a long time coming, and if we don't get this done, well, boy, will there be hell to pay." He gestures out the window. "Look at that crowd."

Polly clears his throat. "Sheriff," he says. "I'm not sure we are sanctioned to proceed as you suggest."

All the men in the room look at him in surprise.

"As the prosecuting attorney, I sought capital punishment in this case. But as a legal scholar, I'd say it's unconstitutional to put Willie Jones back into that chair."

"What are you saying, man?" Roselle demands.

"What I'm saying is this: Willie Jones was tried and convicted of the rape of Grace Sutcliffe. That's an undeniable fact. He was sentenced to die, and tonight, he was brought to the parish jail for that purpose. Everything was done to electrocute this boy up to and including the pulling of the switch and the passing of electricity into his body. You saw it," he says, gesturing toward the chair, askew. "The state failed in its attempt to electrocute him. And so I ask, can the state electrocute a man twice? I don't think so."

"Well, I'll be," Sheriff Roselle says. "If he ain't a nigger lover after all."

Polly shakes his head. "It is a legal matter, sheriff. Not a personal one. It involves our constitutional right of freedom from cruel and unusual punishment. It involves our constitutional right of due process of law and double jeopardy."

"Double jeopardy?"

"Yes. To send Willie back to the chair would consitute double jeopardy. He has already suffered the tortures of death for the same crime. It cannot be repeated."

"I'm afraid that ain't your decision to make."

"No, it's not," Polly admits. "It is one that must be made in a court of law. And until it is, I'd argue that we cannot in good conscience put him back into the chair."

Roselle glares at Polly, his eyes flickering angrily. "You ain't the one in charge here," he says. "I'm going to call the governor."

Ora

Ora sits in the passenger seat of the truck where they've
parked it at the edge of the cemetery, her bare legs pulled
up under her skirt. Outside, Dale and Frank are positioning the
stone for Frank's boy underneath a walnut tree. They work in the
beam of the truck headlights, one with a pick, one with a shovel,
digging a space deep enough in the dirt to hold the tombstone
upright. Tombstones rise like gray teeth from the earth around
them, some crooked and mossy, others newer, adorned with
bouquets of plastic flowers and figurines of angels.

After several minutes, Frank tosses his pick aside, and
Dale stands the shovel in the dirt. They point, exchange words.
Then together they lift the stone from where it waits beneath
the tree and struggle to put it into place. They pack dirt around
the base, pounding it down first with the back of the shovel
and then with their heels. They stand back and look at it together. Then Dale turns away and starts to walk back to the
truck, squinting in the beam of the headlights.

He gets into the truck and shuts the door. Outside, Frank
has crouched down before the stone, his elbows on his knees,
his head in his hands. Dale looks out at him for a moment, then,
as if he can't bear to look anymore, he turns the headlights off.

Ora waits for him to speak. She has given up trying to
understand what he is feeling, tonight. She waits, but he doesn't
speak; he simply stares through the windshield into the night.

"Dale," she says.

He shakes his head.

"No, Dale," she says. "I want to thank you. And I'm sorry for dragging you into things."

Dale shakes his head again.

"You're mad, I know, and I—"

"Not mad," he interrupts her. "Not mad."

"No?"

"Not mad."

"That man out there's the father of the boy—"

"I know who that man is, Ore. You think I'm a fool?"

Ora blinks at him, fumbling to understand.

"That man out there's a father," Dale says. His jaw trembles. "May well be a nigger, but I reckon a father's grief is a father's grief."

Ora hears this and feels an awful knowledge start to burn in her limbs. She swallows, her mouth gone dry. "And what would you know about that?" she asks, combatively, fearfully.

Dale shakes his head.

"Dale?" she demands. She sees a tear run down from the corner of his eye. "Dale? Answer me, Dale!" She pounds his arm with her fist. "What do you know about a father's grief? What do you know?" But she knows what he knows, and the force of it takes her sight away.

"Ora," Dale says, reaching for her.

"No!" she cries, pulling away. "Stop it! Stop it!"

"Ora," he says, "I'm sorry. I'm so sorry." He is weeping, and this time when he reaches for her she doesn't have the energy to resist him.

Lane

Lane stands outside the truck, staring up at the window of the room where a man has just been killed—killed in the brief time between when Lane turned the generator on and then, six designated minutes later, off again. The din of it echoes in his ears. He sits down on the fender and brings his hands to his eyes, despising his own complicity. "Git in the goddamn trailer, trusty!" he hears. He lifts his head; Seward is striding toward him from the jail, his path veering drunkenly despite his apparent determination. "Get in!" The man points as he draws near. Lane stands and climbs into the trailer. "Gimme a hand up," the captain orders, when he's reached the open door.

Lane reaches down and pulls the captain up; Seward's hand is sticky, sweaty, fat. The man pauses to catch his breath in the doorway; each breath sounds nearly like a growl. Outside, the crowd, which had been silent in the execution's aftermath, has begun to mutter. "Git back here with me!" Seward orders. He stalks toward the generator; Lane follows.

"Son of a bitch nigger bastard . . ." Seward shines a flashlight on the side of the generator where the cables are connected.

"What happened?" Lane asks, finally.

"What happened is that son of a bitch didn't die."

Lane gapes.

"Goddamn it," the captain spits. "Hold this." He thrusts the flashlight in Lane's direction. "Shine it here," he commands. Lane obeys, watching as the captain disconnects a wire from one terminal and attaches it to another, his hands trembling. Then Seward stands and turns around. He looks at Lane hard. "Oh, boy," he says, hatred on his face. "You got it coming to you now."

Lane frowns. "What?"

The captain's nostrils flare. "You know what I'm talking about, you insubordinate piece of redneck trash!" The captain leans forward to say this, his face just inches from Lane's. Lane can smell the whiskey on his breath.

"No, I don't, sir."

Seward shakes his head. "You fool," he says. "Puttin' it all on the line for a damn nigger's life."

"I didn't do a thing but what you told me to."

"I didn't tell you to mess with them wires."

"I didn't touch the wires."

Seward gives an incredulous snort. "You saying after all these years I got the wiring wrong? That what you sayin', boy?"

"No," Lane says. "I'm saying I think you couldn't see through the whiskey to get it right." Lane feels a rushing in his limbs, the adrenaline of reckless truth.

Seward's face darkens. "You're in over your head now, trusty," he says. He shakes his head. "Just you wait till the warden gets wind of what you done."

The two lock eyes. Outside, the crowd is now roaring. "Only wish I had," Lane says, at last.

The captain nods, smirks a little. Then he turns, walks to the trailer door, and lowers himself down, stumbling a little as he hits the ground. He gives Lane a final look, then starts back toward the jail, giving a salute of success to the shouting mob beyond.

Lane, stunned, stands inside the trailer where the captain left him. He looks out through the square of the trailer door, window to the world, where Seward is disappearing through the jailhouse door and the people are clamoring for death. It's no world he wants to be a part of. Lane turns to the generator. He tucks the flashlight under his chin, and in that narrow beam of light he does the thing he should have done the first time, the thing he will be blamed for.

Gabe

At first, Gabe doesn't know what is going on. The silence that follows the ceasing of the generator is short-lived; a murmur travels through the solemn crowd like a wave, and soon everyone is jabbering. Arms and fists begin to rise above the mass of heads, and a group in one corner of the green begins to chant a phrase that Gabe can't make out. Someone calls his name, and he looks down.

"Livingstone!" Buddy is calling. "My pa says git down here!"

Buddy is directly at the base of the tree; Pope Crowley, Mr. Cunningham, Sutcliffe, and Amos Hicks are nearby, talking heatedly with a group of other men. One of them is Montgomery. Gabe's hearing goes funny with fear; he doesn't know exactly what he is afraid of, but the feeling is overwhelming. "Livingstone! You hear me?" Buddy is calling.

Gabe shakes his head.

"I said git down here!"

"No! Why? What's going on?"

"You git down here and I'll tell you!" The words are barely out of Buddy's mouth before his father shoves him aside and hauls himself brusquely into the tree, his face rising toward Gabe like something out of a nightmare. He grabs Gabe roughly by the wrist and half carries, half drags him out of the tree; Gabe feels something in his shoulder snap, and he cries out.

"You'd a got down when you were asked I wouldn't have had to pull you out," Mr. Cunningham says, by way of apology. He is out of breath and sweating. "You all right?"

Gabe clutches his shoulder, which throbs with a pain unlike any he's ever felt.

"Chair didn't work," Buddy announces.

Gabe looks at Buddy, astonished even through his agony.

"That's right," Mr. Cunningham says.

Pope Crowley and Montgomery and Amos Hicks and Sutcliffe have turned away from the circle of other men, and stand beside Mr. Cunningham. Their faces look huge to Gabe, so frightening that he nearly forgets his shoulder. "What now?" he asks weakly, looking from Buddy to his father and back to Buddy again, looking at Buddy almost beseechingly. Buddy—an ally if only in age.

"What now depends on whether or not yer daddy has his nigger-lovin way," Montgomery says.

The world begins to whirl around Gabe, voices, bodies, heat, color, noise, as if he were at the center of a horrible gyre. He loses all sense of direction, of right or left, of up or down, and he feels himself begin to fall. Hands catch him before he hits the ground, a rough hand on either arm, and a shocking sear of pain shoots from his shoulder, and the last thing he hears is his own strangled yelp of a cry before everything fizzles out.

Willie

The ceiling seems to move, to zoom in at him then out again, in the same dizzying way the observers seemed to swing in the execution room. Willie shuts his eyes. He lies heavily on the cot in the holding room, his lips throbbing and his limbs tingling with the memory of the current that tore through his body, yet didn't kill him. *I'm not dead,* he thinks. *The chair didn't kill me.*

He'd thought at first that it had killed him, that even in death he could feel the deputies' hands unstrapping him from the chair, the same as it feels when you're alive. They'd moved so quickly, as if they couldn't get him into the grave fast enough, and then the thought of the grave terrified him, if this was what it was to be dead. But then he could stand, he could walk, and as the buzzing in his brain faded, his understanding grew that something had gone wrong, that the chair hadn't killed him after all.

Soon, he hears hushed tones in the corner of the room, and shortly he feels a hand on his. He opens his eyes; Father Hannigan is standing at the edge of the cot. "Willie," the priest says gently.

Willie takes a long breath, in and out.

"How do you feel?"

Willie looks at the ceiling, the gray concrete now holding still. "Tired," he says. He is, overwhelmingly. He would like to sleep forever. He feels the priest's hand tighten around his own.

"They gonna put me back in the chair?" It is an effort to form the words.

"I don't know."

Willie lets his eyes drift from the ceiling to the priest.

"They're calling the governor."

Willie doesn't even try to understand. "They got to put me back in the chair. But this time they got to do it right. I been waitin' so long." He shuts his eyes, and sleep is like an undertow, pulling him irresistibly beneath its surface. He can still hear the sounds of the jail; voices in a nearby room, the scrape of a metal chair leg against the floor as somebody sits down, the slamming of a door. The sound of the crowd outside is a steady thrum, soothing as rain on a tin roof, and then it is rain on a tin roof, the tin roof of his childhood home, where he lies in bed in the early morning, his eyelids heavy with sleep, sealed shut, impossible to open as much as he might will them to, because his mother is waiting for him in the kitchen, then she is not waiting—he can hear her footsteps approaching, hears the door open, hears, "Git up, boy," but it is not his mother's voice. It is the voice of Sheriff Roselle.

Willie forces his eyes open and sees Roselle thrust a pair of handcuffs and shackles toward Sheriff Grazer, who stands in the corner of the room. "Shackle 'im up," Roselle says. "He's going back to Iberia."

PART FOUR

Father Hannigan

When Hannigan drives out of St. Martinville, he does so with the distinct sense that he will never see the town again. He doesn't know why he should feel this; in all likelihood he will be back again in just a few weeks' time, when they put Willie Jones back into the chair. Barring a miracle, Hannigan can't see the execution being stayed, and there are no miracles.

At first Hannigan had thought it was a miracle tonight when Willie survived the chair, but only for a matter of seconds before he began to see it as he sees it now: a cruel trick. Now, Willie must live his last days all over again. His parents will have to suffer the waiting again, too. Hannigan can see them in his mind's eye, holding each other in the darkened doorway of their home after he had given them the news half an hour ago: their boy had survived to die another day.

Hannigan stares straight ahead, where the highway comes at him out of the night. He wishes he could drive right into it, that darkness beyond the ring of his headlights—even as he understands that this is as impossible as it is to step away from your own shadow.

Except, he thinks, that it isn't. Without questioning the impulse, Hannigan snaps the headlights off; immediately he is swallowed up in darkness. He grips the wheel firmly as the car flies through the night; he can see nothing, even as he feels the hot wind of speed pouring in through the open window. He takes a breath and steps more firmly on the gas, his blood rushing with rash exhilaration; the engine roars as the car accelerates, shuddering down the highway. And then, with a lurch that knocks his head against the windshield, it veers off the highway and into the scrub along the side of the road, where finally Hannigan lets the car come to rest.

He sits in the darkness, breathing heavily, as if the car's efforts had been his own. The engine ticks loudly beneath the hood, and the sounds of the night, which had been drowned out by the motor's noise, seem loud in the silence: crickets, an owl, a creature scurrying. Hannigan touches his head on the spot where it hit the windshield and his hand comes away red with blood. He regards his hand dispassionately, and wipes the blood off on his shirt.

When he looks up, he sees a pair of approaching head-lights in the distance, and he hopes that the driver won't see him and stop. He doesn't want to have to explain. He's not sure how he would, and to consider what he's just done nearly makes him laugh; he feels liberated, and also a little bit crazy.

Hannigan is glad when the passing car whizzes by in its own noisy ring of light, and then it is just a pair of taillights fading in the distance. For a moment, Hannigan watches after it. Then he turns, starts his own engine, and steers the car carefully back onto the road.

Nell

Mother's eyes are open when Nell goes to her shortly after midnight. At first Nell worries that she might have died, but then she sees her blink, sees the gentle rise of breath beneath the sheet. She stands at the bedside, looking down at the woman—her head nearly lost in the pillow, her white hair feathering around her rawboned face, and her eyes blue, clear, open, staring. Nell wonders what Mother sees. She wonders if Mother even knows that she is there.

After a minute, Nell turns to leave, but something stops her—the same mysterious impulse that drove her to come there in the first place; she doesn't ordinarily pay a midnight visit to the room. But tonight, she was compelled to by something in her bones, just as now she feels compelled to stay, and so she pulls a chair to the bedside and sits down in the darkness. She gazes at her mother-in-law's profile, the fine, sloped nose bone, the broad forehead, the deep plunge of the open eye. She wonders at this wakefulness, wonders how many hours at night the woman spends awake, and alone, trapped in her ravaged body. She hopes tonight is an aberration; perhaps, she thinks, Mother is aware of more than they realize. Perhaps she is awake for the same reason Nell is.

"Mother," she begins, and she takes the woman's hand in her own. "Mother, I don't know if you can hear me, but the thing's been done." She pauses, takes a breath. "It's after midnight, now, so the thing's been done, and a boy's been put to death." She feels a wave of emotion come over her, a sharp ache in her throat. "And I was part of it. There I was, here I am, right in the thick of it." She squeezes Mother's hand, yearning for some response. There is none. "There's another me somewhere, you know," Nell goes on. "Somewhere north, maybe New York City. She's an artist, wouldn't tolerate this sort of thing for all the world. She's lucky; she doesn't have to." Nell blinks, feeling herself on the backside of the wave, riding it swiftly into weariness. She lets go of Mother's hand and sits back. "But," she says softly, "she doesn't have Gabe."

Gabe

G abe wakes up in the backseat of a moving car, and a moan escapes him, unbidden. He feels a body shift beside his; Pope Crowley is looking down at him.

"He's awake," Pope comments. No one in the car responds.

It is not the car that Gabe rode in to St. Martinville, and it's not the same company. Pope Crowley and Sutcliffe are here, but Buddy is gone, Mr. Cunningham is gone, Amos Hicks is gone. They have been replaced by Montgomery and two other men who are unfamiliar to Gabe, and there is yet another man standing on the running board.

"Where are we going?" Gabe asks, looking fearfully into the darkness outside.

"Shut up," one of the unfamiliar men snaps.

"I betch you'd like to know," Pope Crowley drawls at the same time. He shifts again in his seat, knocking against Gabe's shoulder.

"Ah!" Gabe hollers. He clutches at his shoulder, crippled by the radiating pain.

"Arm's least of your concerns, boy." This is the second unfamiliar man, who is driving.

"What're you gonna do to me?" Gabe asks. He is crying, out of pain, out of fear, out of remorse. No one answers him, and when he looks up at Pope Crowley the man won't meet his eyes. "What are you gonna do to me?" Gabe asks again, desperately. "Please don't hurt me! I'll do anything you say!" He looks desperately from Crowley on his one side to the unknown man on his other side. But neither of them responds. In the front passenger seat, Sutcliffe turns his head, casts a brief, impenetrable glance Gabe's way.

"I'll do anything you say," Gabe repeats, though he doesn't know what he could possibly do for these men, doesn't even know what he's done to displease them, except for being who he is: his father's son. "Anything you say," he manages again. He slumps into himself in terrified defeat, crying openly, and then, with the instinct of a child, he buries his face and weeps against Pope Crowley's thigh.

Polly

When he comes into the kitchen he finds the lights off, the room empty. He crosses the tiles to the sink to wash his hands, and then he bends down and starts to splash handfuls and handfuls of cold water against his face. Finally, without unbending himself, he reaches up and turns the tap off, and then he just rests there, his elbows on the sink edge and his wet forehead in his fingertips.

After some time, he stands. He dries his face on his sleeve and looks around the dark room. He is tired, yet feels too jittery to sleep, and so he takes a seat at the kitchen table, where he sits in darkness, his hands in fists on the tabletop, his mind blank.

He hasn't been there long when Nell comes into the room. She sits down across from him without turning on the light, but she says nothing. She just looks at him, and waits.

He meets her gaze. "He's still alive," he says.

There's a pause. Then: "I don't understand." Nell says it slowly, cautiously, as if she were being tricked. "What do you mean, he's still alive?"

Polly tells her in detail about the writhing and straining, the puffed lips, the whole ugly ordeal. "And then, after all that, they wanted to rewire the chair and try it again," he says.

"But they didn't?"

Polly shakes his head. "No," he says.

"What stopped them?"

Polly takes a deep breath, looks at his hands on the table, then lowers them into his lap. "You can't punish someone for the same crime twice. That's double jeopardy. It's not my opinion. It's a right."

Nell says nothing. She looks at him expectantly.

"But it was the governor who stopped it officially. Said it would appear *in bad taste* to put him back in the chair tonight."

Nell frowns. "So what happens now?"

Polly takes another deep breath. "I expect they'll try it again at a later date."

Nell frowns, leaning forward again. "How can they? What about double jeopardy?"

Polly shakes his head in defeat. "It'd be a tough fight."

"Well, can't you try?"

Polly looks at his wife, dismayed. "I can't. No. Maybe someone else can. Maybe someone else will. But I can't."

"Why on earth not?"

"Nell, I'm the elected district attorney. Willie's prosecutor. I sought the chair in the first place."

"So? Resign! You can do that. Fight the tough fight. Here's your chance to make a difference!"

Polly looks at her seriously. "Nell," he says. "If I did that, what do you think they'd do to Gabe?"

Nell does not respond. She blinks, presses a fist against her lips.

Polly reaches across the table for her hand. He looks at her searchingly, yearning to say something. But he doesn't know how to express it, the swirling mess of guilt and gratefulness and love and fear and doubt spiraling through his body, so they sit there in the darkness, holding each other's hands.

Gabe

After lurching down a bumpy dirt road for several minutes, the car comes to an abrupt halt. Gabe is thrown forward into the back of the driver's seat, and barely enough time has passed for him to fall to the floor before he feels his collar tighten as he's yanked roughly out of the car and to the ground. He is only distantly aware now of the pain in his shoulder, which, though his arm hangs wrong from its socket, has ceased to matter. All he wants is to live. He lies on his back in field grass, looking up at Pope Crowley's face above him, which appears upside down, the man's features casting shadows across his face in the light coming from within the car. Pope is breathing heavily. The other men have climbed out of the car, too, and gather around them.

"Drag him in the field," Gabe hears a voice say, and Pope's face gets closer, bigger, as the man bends down to grab Gabe's collar again.

Gabe lets his body go limp as Pope drags him through the grasses, the hard nodes of their stems sharp against his back. The fabric of his collar rips, and his upper body hits the ground only for a moment before Pope grabs his wrist and begins to drag him by the arm instead. The other men follow, dark silhouettes against the fading light from the car. Gabe shuts his eyes, and then there is no pain, no sight, just the tromping noise of footsteps and the rustling of the grass. He feels tired, so tired; all his body wants is to give in to sleep, but he wills himself to listen to the footsteps, to listen to the grass, to focus on the now as if doing so will make it impossible to die.

After several minutes, he feels himself being released into the grass. He can hear the men circle around him, can hear their breathing. He opens his eyes, sees their dark faces around him, feels a drop of Pope's sweat hit his face. And then a boot to his side takes his breath away. He shuts his eyes again and curls into a ball, his arms around his head, and waits for more, which comes. Boot after boot batters his body, and he accepts the pain, focuses only on life, on life, on life. If he can stay awake, he will not die. This is what he tells himself. He must stay awake.

And he does. After some time, he is vaguely aware that the boots have ceased. He does not move. He does not open his eyes. He lies like a rag doll in the grass, on his back, uncurled in the beating. Someone clears his throat and spits. Someone else coughs. All of the men pant heavily. And then they walk away: fading footsteps through the grass. Only when Gabe hears the car engine in the distance does he open his eyes—or the eye that is not swollen shut. He tries to lift his hand to the swollen eye, but his arm won't move. Nothing will move; his body is broken in the grass. Around him, the tall blades rise against the sky, and Gabe has never seen so many stars, dense, glowing clusters of them, more than he'd ever think imaginable, which, to his amazement, start to fall toward him, a shower of stars so beautiful it makes Gabe want to cry.

Father Hannigan

His head is still bleeding when he gets back to the rectory. His whole skull has started to ache—a deep throbbing like in the aftermath of hard tears. He shuts the rectory door behind him and sets the car keys on the table by the door, where he also drops his pocket rosary and collar, gratefully unfastened from around his neck.

He passes through the darkness to the bathroom, where he flips the light switch and waits as the fluorescent light comes on, flicker by brighter flicker until the room is a garish white. He looks into the mirror above the sink; for a brief moment, he can hardly recognize himself. It isn't the blood on his head, and it isn't the weariness etched into his face; it is a fundamental lack of recognition, as if he were looking at a stranger. Childishly, despite himself, Hannigan lifts a hand; the reflection in the mirror does the same.

He cleans the gash on his forehead with toilet paper soaked in iodine, which stings more than the wound itself, and when he takes the paper away the wound is clear for only a second before blood begins again to weep through the bone-white underflesh. There is nothing in the medicine cabinet aside from his razor and some shaving cream, and so he fashions his own bandage of toilet paper, which he folds into a neat square and brings with him to the living room, where he finds a roll of Scotch tape in the desk drawer. He tapes the fat white square down over his wound, carefully smoothing each piece of tape against his skin. And then he just stands there, unsure what next to do with himself, the trajectory of his night abruptly over. Sleep seems impossible.

He gazes at the telephone on the desk, wishing he had somebody to call. He blinks, lets his eyes travel to the coffee table, where the whiskey and the glass are sitting as he left them. Waiting there for him, and suddenly in his eyes they are the only thing in the room, calling him as they've been calling him all day, all week, for years. This time, tonight, he obeys.

Frank

Sometime after two o'clock, Frank gets out of bed. Elma is sleeping, so he rises gently from the mattress, gathers up his clothing, and goes quietly into the other room. He gets dressed in the kitchen, his mind buzzing with the knowledge that Willie is alive. Willie is alive. Willie is alive. He accepts this in the same way he has accepted all of the day's improbable events, questioning nothing. He figures everything happens for a reason. Still, as he ties the laces of his shoes, his hands shake, shake with the same astonishment and wonder that earlier, when the priest came with the news, sent Elma to her knees.

Elma. He looks toward the bedroom door, where he can make out the corner of the bed where Elma is sleeping. He hesitates for a moment, then walks softly to the door. He stands on the threshold, his shadow long across Elma's still body, finally, after so many wakeful nights, asleep. Frank blinks at her, thinking how much younger she looks in sleep, her worry lines smoothed, her frown softened into a gentle arc. Things will be different now, he thinks. Willie is alive, and if so by the grace of God, he can't see that grace falling away. Eighteen years ago, against all odds, Willie was born, and tonight, against all odds, he was saved. He had to have been saved for a reason. This is what Frank believes.

He takes a breath and goes out the back kitchen door to the small outbuilding where he keeps his tools and the mule. Kept the mule. He looks into Bess's empty stall, the trampled hay on the dirt floor, where he knows Grace and Willie sometimes lay. Tomorrow he will have to go back to the field where he left the mule and do something with her body. What, he doesn't know.

For now, he finds the sledgehammer among his tools, resting up against the wall. It hasn't been used in some time, and it is heavier than he remembers. Cobwebs have gathered in the L where the head meets the lever. Frank wipes the fine filaments away with his hand, remembering how Willie had trailed him all those years ago as he drove fence posts into the ground around the Harkness place, post after post under a white-hot sun. It's funny; Frank remembers distinctly the sound of the metal head against the wood against the ground, a deeply satisfying combination of thunk and thud.

Tonight, he hoists the sledgehammer over his shoulder and goes out into the night, passing around the house and out to the street. It is quiet. In the middle of the night, it should be, but the stillness is striking given the earlier crowd; he'd half expected to find angry folks out in the street, but he doesn't see a soul. The only sign of life is the occasional lit window, and a single mangy dog who follows him for a quarter mile down the street.

It doesn't take long for Frank to reach the cemetery where just hours ago he readied Willie's stone. It stands, smooth and unengraved, in the moonlight among the other stones. The walnut tree stands quietly above, the green balls of its ready nuts hanging or fallen on the ground; one, since Frank was here earlier, has come to rest along the base of Willie's stone. Frank gazes down at the nut, and at the stone.

The stone. He could save it, he thinks, use it for Elma or himself when their time comes. Or maybe he could sell it; though he doubts that he could return it for his borrowed funds. But the stone is the marker of an unrealized and undeserved death. That is why he is here. So he lifts the sledgehammer over his head, and with all the strength he has he drives it crashing down.

Dale

When they get back to the station, Dale pulls the Bantam into the garage and cuts the engine. He turns to reach for Ora's hand, but she has already opened the truck door, which hangs open behind her even after she has leaped to the ground and disappeared outside. Dale sits for a minute in the dark garage. Then he reaches across the seat and shuts the passenger door before getting out himself and easing the door closed behind him. He gets the .22 from the back of the truck and goes outside. Across the lot, Benny sits in his truck, watching; Dale can see the reflection of dashboard lights in his eyes.

Dale turns and starts to walk across the lot toward the station. Halfway there, he notices the dog standing warily in the shadows, and starts to approach him; the dog tucks his tail and sidles away. Dale frowns; that he should inspire such fear in the animal fills him with a deep sense of shame. He squats down and offers his hand, then remembers the rifle, and how earlier the dog had cowered at its end. And so he slides the rifle away from him, across the dirt. He calls to the dog gently; and cautiously, lured by Dale's outstretched hand, the dog comes.

For several minutes, Dale squats there in the dirt and strokes the dog, between his ears, down the knobs of his spine, along the thick muscle of his neck. He thinks of nothing but the feel of the furred flesh beneath his palms, and beneath that the warm workings of life.

When he stands, the dog shudders off his touch, then follows him around the station to the back kitchen door. Dale lets the screen door close behind him. He flicks the light on and goes to the cabinet for two bowls; one he fills with water, the other with stew left over from dinner tonight. Dinner: it seems a lifetime ago. The dog stands at the door, his head lowered as he watches Dale through the screen, and when he sees Dale coming with the bowls, he backs away, turns a hungry circle in the dirt.

Dale sets the dishes on the ground. Then he goes back into the kitchen and gazes down the hallway. The door to their bedroom is open, and he can see that the room is empty. The door to Tobe's room is closed. He walks quietly in that direction, and pauses outside the door. Then he taps on the door with his knuckle. There is no response.

"Ora," he calls softly. "Ora, you in there?"

Again, there is no response.

"Ora," he calls, a little more loudly, and taps on the door again.

Still nothing, so he tries the handle. The door is locked.

"Ora, can I come in?"

Silence. For a minute, Dale stands outside the door, as lonely as if he were the last person left in the world. Then he moves back down the hallway to the kitchen, where he puts the dishes from dinner away, taking them two by two from where Ora has set them to dry in the rack. Just as dinner seems a lifetime ago, so does morning seem a lifetime away.

He feels lost in a purgatory of endless night; his hands are trembling, and he nearly drops two bowls.

He looks toward the door, where the dog has finished eating and is watching him again through the screen. Dale goes to the door and pushes it open, invites the dog inside. The animal sniffs around the corners of the kitchen, and when Dale leaves the room and goes back down the hallway, the dog follows, stops when Dale does again outside Tobe's door.

He doesn't knock, this time. He doesn't call Ora's name. Instead he sits down in the hall outside the door, leans against the wall. The dog explores their bedroom briefly, then returns to Dale and curls up on the floor beside him. Dale puts a hand on the animal, and shuts his eyes. Until Ora is ready, he will stay here, and he will wait.

Lane

They drive back the way they came, passing through the flat fields of sugarcane, the leaves and stalks flashing along the periphery of Lane's vision, through the vast black sea of the prairie, through the Atchafalaya swampland, where the great-kneed cypress and tupelo rise from the water around them, dark shapes against the dark sky. This time, Seward drives; Lane sits in the passenger seat, cuffs around his wrists and shackles around his legs. He watches as the truck weaves from one side of the road to the other, steered by the captain's unsteady hand. Lane doesn't care. He doesn't care if Seward runs the truck off the road, if it kills him. His eyes are heavy, and he lets himself drift into and out of sleep, his head snapping upright just as his chin has landed on his chest. Images float by like dreams: a wheat field, the waitress, snakes and wires, the dog he'd had as a kid. He drifts, wondering whether this is what it's like to die.

A change in the truck's momentum brings him back to the present moment, and he sits upright as the captain makes the hard turn off the state highway onto the gravel road that leads down to the Angola ferry. The sky has started to fade from black to blue, the world to reappear; Lane can see into the boggy land around them, the forest rising from the wetland. The black shapes of trees take on detail as the sky behind them grows lighter, and the neon film of pollen on the surface of the water glows.

Finally the road deposits them on the banks of the Mississippi, where the ferry is waiting, tailgate lowered and ready to accept the load it sent forth nearly twenty-four hours ago. The crew greets them wordlessly, goes about the solemn work of tying, untying, pushing off, and starting out over the swirling brown water toward the east, where Angola waits. The ferry makes its way across the river, and with it the truck and the chair and the five men, three outside the truck and two within, all of them watching as the sun crests the horizon and the undersides of the clouds begin to smolder.

Willie

And, in his cell, Willie is awake for sunrise, too. Through the ten bars of his window, he watches the backside of the sky as it lightens into yet another day.

Acknowledgments

Although *The Mercy Seat* is a work of fiction, it was inspired by real events. The character of Willie Jones is loosely based on two people: Willie McGee, who was accused of raping a white woman and put to death in Mississippi's traveling electric chair in 1951, and Willie Francis, who was accused of killing a white man and whose failed execution in 1946 was successfully reattempted in 1947.

The death warrant and formal death decree read before each execution in the novel are taken from the historical record of Willie Francis's execution. Polly's argument against a second attempt at execution is the same reasoning attempted by Willie Francis's lawyer, Bertrand de Blanc. The towns and cities referenced in the novel are real, as is Gruesome Gertie. Ultimately eighty-seven people were executed in the chair.

The following books and sources were invaluable to my research: *The Execution of Willie Francis: Race, Murder, and the Search for Justice in the American South* by Gilbert King, *The Eyes of Willie McGee: A Tragedy of Race, Sex, and Secrets in the Jim Crow South* by Alex Heard, *Laurel Remembrances* by Cleveland Payne, *Dangerous Liaisons: Sex and Love in the Segregated South* by Charles F. Robinson II, *Coming of Age in Mississippi* by Anne Moody, and the article "The History of New Iberia" by Glenn R. Conrad.

I am grateful to the following people for their inspiration, knowledge, and support: Adin Murray, who introduced me to *The Radio Diaries Podcast: Willie McGee and the Travelling Electric Chair*. Kate Levine, who answered my endless legal questions, and Leslie Starritt, who carefully corrected my southern dialect. I am indebted to Endicott College, whose support allowed me the time to work on the book. I feel lucky to have Amanda Urban as my faithful agent, and Elisabeth Schmitz as my incredibly wise, insightful, and supportive editor. Thanks also to careful readers Katie Raissian, Corinna Barsan, and Carole Welch.

And as always, nothing means as much as the support and encouragement of my parents, my sisters, and my husband, Adin.